OF DREAMS AND MOSSLIGHT

A.J. NORA

LION BRIAR BOOKS LLC

To request permission, contact the publisher at aj@ajnorabooks.com

Paperback: 978-1-967056-06-4

Ebook: 978-1-967056-05-7

First paperback edition October 2025

Edited by: Atwater Group

Cover Art by: GetCovers

Lion Briar Books

ajnorabooks.com

AUTHOR'S NOTE

This is a closed door queer normative portal fantasy romance.

I believe in representation, and I will always include queer people in my stories because we exist and deserve to see ourselves in the novels we read.

If you'd like content warnings, please head to my website https://ajnorabooks.com/content-warnings-for-kingdoms-of-kaelums/ (to get the list.)

Thank you for supporting an indie author. I hope you enjoy! <3

If you'd like to join my newsletter list, you can do so at https://dashboard.mailerlite.com/forms/1224485/158024175059994284/share to stay up to date on upcoming books and other exciting news!

SILVIS
THE SOMNIUM SEA
KHENT
DAES RIVER
DREAMER RIVER
SINK FALLS
KAESY
SILVER MOUNTAINS
SHEEPSGROVE FOREST
THE ABYSSAL BAY
HOLLOW DESERT
UVIEL
THE CAPITAL
QUEEN'S CREEK
CAINE
SEAI
MAJESTY MARSH
Nord

For my mom, who loves me as I am.

PRONUNCIATION GUIDE

Silvis: SIL-vis

Brynia:BRI-nee- yah

Anastasia Behar: An-NUH-stay-zuh Bay-HAR

Meredith Kaesy: Mare-UH-dith KAY-see

Alixandra Bludeg: Al-ix-AN-dra BLU-deg

Creon: KREE-on

Vasileios Maeb-Somni: Va-ssee'-lee-os Mahb-SOM-nee

Shiloh Leigdraca: SHY-low Lē(d)zh-DRA-ca

THE STORY SO FAR

Four years ago, Lana's mother disappeared. When the monsters from her nightmares seem to appear outside her work, she decides to finally investigate her mother's disappearance. While looking through her mother's room, Lana realizes that her mother left for the faerie realm, a place she didn't know existed. Determined to find her mother, Lana decides to wait for night and confront the shadows, with the hope of jumping through one of their portals to finally find her mother.

Night comes, but so does her best friend Liam. Together, they escape the monsters by following a stranger, Shiloh, through a portal to faerie. Shiloh says he can help find her mother. However, Liam isn't suited to the faerie world and immediately falls unconscious.

Lana, Liam, Shiloh, and his horse Lu make their way to a temple in the desert, where Shiloh says they are safe from the Hollows. Lana finds out she has a sister named Anastasia. Another secret her mother kept. But her sister is in a magical sleep, and Shiloh thinks Lana can wake her! Lana tries, but instead of waking Anastasia, she's sucked inside her.

Lana wakes up in Anastasia's body and decides to explore the temple while Shiloh sleeps. While exploring the temple, she meets Vas, a strange fae seeking refuge in the temple, and he joins their journey, despite Shiloh's protests. What she doesn't know is that Vas is a fae prince who once loved her sister.

The Hollows attack the temple, and the trio are forced down a spiral hatch into the underground, where Lana sees Haven for the first time. Shiloh falls unconscious from overuse of magic, leaving Vas and Lana alone in the dark cavern at the base of the spiraling stairs.

Sitting together in the cavern, Vas has a realization. Lana might be his fated mate. But he can't tell her yet. He doesn't quite believe it's true. How can she be his mate if he loves her sister? Meanwhile, Lana has finally decided to confess her feelings for her best friend Liam — that is, if he ever wakes up again.

CHAPTER I

Lana

The city of Haven nestled in the center of an enormous cavern, where shadows stretched and lingered, only momentarily broken by the twinkling blue of bioluminescent moss that grew in sporadic patches on the distant ceiling and stony walls. It was a city of perpetual night, a fact that kept Lana on edge as she sat at the bottom of the winding stone staircase that was the entrance to the cavern. Lana hope they were safe beneath the desert, but the Hollows could be anywhere, hiding in the dark city.

At least a mile walk and a rushing river separated her from the city of stone skyscrapers and stained glass that loomed in the distance. An icy breeze swept around her, rustling her blonde hair, and she shivered, wishing she had something more than her sister's old tunic and armor to wear.

The city skyline seemed so much like those from her home in the human realm—the mundane realm, as Shiloh had called it. But the Court of Dreams wasn't her home, even though it had apparently been her mother's. *She kept so many secrets*, Lana thought as she looked down at her calloused hands.

These hands didn't belong to her. She clasped her fingers together, stretching the joints that still ached to move. This body had been asleep for decades, part of a spell her mother and Shiloh had worked to put up a wall, trapping the monsters terrorizing the fae. *Another of my mother's secrets.* A flash of anger rushed up, but Lana pushed it down, smothering it in the dark corners of her mind. *She had her reasons. She must have. Why else would she not tell me about my sister?*

Sister. The word bounced around her mind. Anastasia was her sister, but their souls were trapped in the same body, or at least partially. Lana still didn't understand it, and Shiloh seemed to have no desire to explain anything he knew—not that he could at the moment, as he'd fallen unconscious after they'd entered the cavern.

He had pressured her into trying to break the spell on Anastasia, spewing nonsense about how she was the key, that somehow she was special, important, but that had backfired and now Anastasia was still asleep and according to Shiloh, her soul wasn't even intact. Only part of it lived in this body and the rest? His best guess was that it was in the amulet her mother wore, so that was their goal — to find the amulet and her mother to wake Anastasia, who could defeat the Hollows, and then Lana and her best friend, Liam, could go home to Feyville.

Liam was in the city somewhere. After stepping through the portal, he'd fallen unconscious. When Lana woke up in her sister's body, Shiloh said that Liam and her body were both in his home here in Haven, but with Shiloh unconscious, she did not know where to look.

At least Vas was here with her. Lana looked over at the quiet fae man, who sat staring at the city with a yearning expression. With his white hair, pointed ears, and stone gray skin, Vas was undeniably fae. His hair hung in messy curls and tangled at the base of his dark, ram-like horns, which jutted from his skull behind his ears. Despite his otherworldliness, he felt familiar to Lana. She decided it must be his eyes, bright green like Liam's, that made her feel so comfortable around him.

They sat in companionable silence, waiting for Shiloh to rouse. Hours had passed already, and their only guide through the brilliant but empty city was still unconscious. Lana jerked at every noise, imagining the Hollows careening down the staircase behind her or appearing in the murky shadows that surrounded them.

"Shiloh said the city was abandoned," Vas said, breaking the silence with the deep rumble of his voice. "But it still seems so alive."

Lana nodded. Moss grew. The river rushed, singing its song into the echoing stone. Bugs crawled along the damp ground.

An entire forest of strange mushrooms grew in the distance at the mouth of the river. For a city without people, it still lived and breathed.

"So, where do you live in Haven?" Vas sat cross-legged on the ground, turning his head towards her with a curious tilt.

"I don't live there." Lana averted her gaze, picking at a loose thread on her trousers. "I'm not really from around here."

"But—" Vas cut himself off and turned around fully to look at her. His brows furrowed.

"It's complicated."

"Just like how it's complicated that you're related to Anastasia?"

"Yes," she said curtly. She wanted to trust him with the whole truth, but everything about the last day had made her wary. When had she ever been the type to follow strangers through portals or fight monsters?

"Don't you think we should just try to make it to the city?" She asked, rocking back and forth with nervous energy. She and Vas had discussed their options after Shiloh had fainted. Waiting seemed to be the prudent thing to do. The bags Shiloh carried had plenty of water, but as time marched on, Lana grew anxious.

"He's the only one that knows the way through the city. I still think we should wait," Vas said.

"We've been waiting," she said with an exasperated sigh. "We're out in the open. If the Hollows show up..." she trailed off, not wanting to think of the bloodbath that would surely happen. "What if Shiloh is seriously in trouble? He could be on his deathbed, and we're just waiting for something to happen."

Lana slid over to Shiloh and started patting his cheek. A spark of anxiety jolted through her body, tightening around her throat and squeezing her lungs. They were alone in the dark—the most dangerous place she could be. The only person who knew where to go was unconscious or dying. *Trapped.* Her breath turned shallow as she struggled to breathe through her panic.

"And what if we move him and that kills him? Or we go into the city to more Hollows? It's safer here until he wakes up," Vas said, though his voice wavered with uncertainty as he watched Lana.

She ignored him and kept patting Shiloh's cheek. "Wake up." Her gentle pats grew stronger and more insistent as she chanted her plea: "Wake. Up." The sound of her hand slapping his bare cheek cut through the silence of the oppressive dark.

"Stop," Vas said softly.

But she didn't.

"Stop it," he said again.

Still, she didn't.

Vas moved to her side and reached for her hand. "Lana, please."

She didn't pull away as he grasped her shaking hand in his. The warmth of his skin comforted her, but her thoughts continued to spiral. "I can't keep waiting like this. I don't want to be here anymore." *What would have happened if she hadn't thrown herself into the fight with the Hollow earlier? Would Vas have gotten hurt? Would he have fought off the creatures on his own, without needing Shiloh to intervene? If she had just stayed out of it, would Shiloh have used so much magic? Would he have collapsed like this? Would she even be here if she'd gone with Liam that night? Was Liam okay?*

Vas squeezed her hand. "Alright. It's alright." He looked across the city. The pale blue of mosslight illuminated his silhouette.

With her hand wrapped in his, she felt the tightness slowly relax. Deliberately, she took slow, deep breaths. Lana and Vas sat in silence together, listening to the distant river and the gentle rush of their own breath.

His fingers twitched against her skin and she was suddenly aware of how close they were sitting and the unfamiliar warmth that coiled in her stomach, like flaming butterflies, ready to burn her alive. His arm brushed against hers and her heart stuttered.

Why did she feel like this? It was entirely abnormal. Well... Her face heated with a flush as she remembered the only other time she'd felt like this had been one late night watching the stars pop into existence with Liam, but that was before her mother had disappeared. But Vas wasn't Liam. In fact, she barely knew the fae sitting beside her. Could it be that her feelings weren't her own?

Lana closed her eyes and felt through the dark recesses of her mind, looking for the sister she'd never known, but whose body she now inhabited in the fae realm. *Anastasia?* She whispered in her mind, but no words greeted her, only the same golden fire that swirled in her palm and along her skin where Vas touched.

"Vas," she breathed, turning her gaze to his in the dim of the cavern. Even in the dark, she could see the bright green of his eyes as he met her stare. A thought—no, a memory–niggled in the back of her mind, desperate to be remembered. Who was he?

"Yes?" he asked in a whisper.

"How did you know Anastasia?"

His eyes widened and then dimmed as he turned towards Haven again. "She was..." he sighed, trailing off.

"Were you two lovers?" Lana dared to ask, pulling her hand gently from his.

He dropped his palm into his lap and ran his thumb across his fingers. "L-lovers?" a nervous laugh escaped his lips. "No. Nothing like that," he said, but his voice held a note of sadness. "We only met once, at a ball. She was the first—the only, actually–person to ever dance with me besides my tutors. She..." he trailed off again and shook his head.

"You're in love with her…"

"What?" Vas spluttered, but his cheeks darkened with a blush. "I'd only just met her." He didn't deny it, which was answer enough for Lana, and considering how his proximity ignited strange feelings in her body, Lana felt certain that Anastasia felt something for him, too.

"A ball…" Flashes of red and gold bubbled to her consciousness, gauzy fabrics. A young man, standing alone in a corner ignored by everyone else. Lana blinked away the haze of Anastasia's memories. Ignored in a corner. He must have not been an important noble, Lana thought to herself, but before she could ask him about it, Vas spoke.

"Are you still wanting to head into the city, even though our guide is unconscious?" he asked, clearly changing the subject. She sighed, trying to shake off the strange feeling Anastasia had left her with and turned her attention to the city.

Haven stretched before them, ruined and empty, but Lana didn't feel safe sitting at the base of the stairs in the deep shadows of the cave without the comforting blue glow of the mosslight lanterns. She imagined shapes in the dimness, hungry jaws and glowing red eyes. It would be safer in the city.

"Yes," she said.

Vas exhaled deeply and stood, brushing himself off. It was clear in the way he moved his shoulder ached and he was exhausted. Despite that, he stooped down and pulled Shiloh up onto his back, wincing at the effort.

"Let's go," he said.

Lana looked up at him for a moment before pushing up from the ground to stand beside him. He was hurt. Despite her fear, she couldn't let him walk at the front. Lana steeled herself against her decision and said, "since I have the sword, I'll lead."

Vas huffed through his nose with amusement. "We're both vulnerable, no matter who goes first, but lead on, brave warrior." He grinned at her, playfully flashing his sharp canines.

She rolled her eyes at him, unable to help from returning his smile, and then walked forward, navigating down the dark hillside toward a path that wound across the empty landscape of the cavern and toward the city. The sword was once again sheathed at her side, and she felt strong as she walked the path down, her feet moving with a certainty that she didn't feel.

CHAPTER 2

Lana

Worn stone brick made up the road, which was lined with tall lamps made of the same brick. Marble and other assorted stone twisted into the lamps, as if the structures had risen from the ground itself and taken shape. Upon closer inspection, Lana noticed the blue glow that emanated from the lanterns was created by the same moss from the ceiling, but tied in intricate knots.

They walked in silence, their attention captivated by the cavern and the city, until they stopped at the edge of the river that spanned from one side of the cavern to the other. A stone bridge spanned the river, arching up over the dark rushing waters. Just before the bridge, an enormous archway stood, marking the entrance to Haven.

The glow of the moss lanterns illuminated the archway clearly, where words were scrawled across the stone. Lana squinted, trying to make sense of the symbols, which felt familiar, but she couldn't force them into making sense.

"Haven," Vas said, "for the Children of Flame."

"The Children of Flame?" Lana could only imagine that had something to do with the fiery magic that she'd seen Shiloh use.

"There are old stories that talk about Haven's founding by a man named Flame. Every place has a founding myth, I suppose, but it's nothing I've ever been forced to study," Vas said with a shrug as he moved toward the entryway, hesitating. "I've never been to Haven, but I had hoped to once." He seemed far off in thought.

He stepped forward, past the archway and smiled, continuing onto the bridge. Lana followed, staring at the dark water. When she took her first steps onto the bridge, the rippling surface of the water bubbled before golden light floated to the surface like fireflies. Vas kept walking, unaware of whatever was happening in the river.

As Lana moved forward, the light moved with her, dancing across the obsidian water. After they had all crossed the bridge, the lights drifted back down into the depths. The golden light had warmed the cool tones of the cave, but now they were once more surrounded by the dim shadows and blue glow of mosslight.

They continued down the path, drawing nearer to the cityscape. The buildings loomed high, towering above them. In the pale light, the stone seemed to glow white, like the full moon.

Vas stopped, taking a deep breath. Sweat dripped down his forehead and his face twisted into a pained grimace.

Shiloh still limply draped across Vas's shoulders. Lana grabbed Shiloh's hand, where it dangled near Vas's cheek. "I'll take him for a while," she said.

He shook his head slightly. "I've got him."

"Just let me."

"No. You scout. I'll deal with him." His words were short and quick as he took deep breaths between each word.

"Why don't we rest for a minute?"

Vas gave her an intense look. His green eyes pierced hers, and they shared a quiet yet stubborn battle of wills in that moment.

With another deep breath and a quick exhale, Vas succumbed and gestured to a small building nearby. They were still on the outskirts of Haven, but just ahead, a small building stood. It looked to have been a stable, which baffled Lana. Underground horses wasn't something she'd been expecting, but then again everything about this city, and about the fae realm, seemed both familiar and fantastic, so who was she to question the logic of Haven?

Lana, being pacified, nodded and led the way. The ambience of the cave felt deafening as she approached the small stable. The dripping of water and gurgling of the river mixed with the occasional shifting rocks and their own echoing footsteps.

Lana made her way carefully around the entrances, stealing glances into the windows where she could, though they were difficult to see through. The windows of the stable—and from a distance, it seemed most of the ones in the city as well—were made of stained glass. The mosaic of color obscured and muddled whatever image she might have had of the rooms beyond them.

She wasn't sure what she had expected, but when she finally slipped beyond the large double doors of the stable, she saw it was empty. Or at least, almost entirely empty.

Stalls lined the walls closest to the entrance and there seemed to be rooms off to the side that held supplies, or perhaps even bedrooms. She walked slowly along the stalls, noting the bareness. The floors weren't littered with hay. All the troughs were empty of everything but thick layers of dust. She found it all strange.

Saddles and bridles withered away, cracked leather and molding fabrics. Lana grazed her fingers across one saddle and her finger came away with a layer of dust that she quickly brushed off on her pants.

At the end of the hall, she noticed a large, dark lump tucked away into the last stall. As she approached, her breath caught. The dark lump was a horse. A beautiful, black horse that curled upon itself in a motionless sleep.

"Oh," Vas said softly as his own eyes fell on the horse.

Lana frowned and covered her mouth with her hand as she continued to approach. She didn't want to believe what was so obvious. How did Shiloh's horse get down here? And long before they ever did? Shiloh had told her that his associate had taken her body and Liam down to Haven, but was this what he'd meant? Someone must have used the horse to transport Liam and her body.

The horse's coat gleamed unnaturally, casting light like a mirror. She hesitantly placed her hand on the horse's neck and quickly yanked back in surprise at the slick coldness of the beast. It had no breath and held no warmth, but at her touch, the beast's eyes slid open.

Its warm brown gaze fell on her, and with a soft huff of acknowledgment, the beast stood. The horse's movements tinkled like bells, muscles moving in a kaleidoscope of shadow. It had to be magic—a magical glass stallion. It was enormous, unfolding up to its full height. It was larger than any horse Lana had ever seen—bigger even than the Shire horse she'd seen when she'd gone with Liam's family on vacation back in sixth grade.

Lana stumbled backward, away from the beast, but it stood still and silent. The blue light glinted across its glass-like hide.

"Lu?" Lana asked, remembering the name Shiloh had called the creature as it carried her through the desert.

The horse flared its nostrils slightly, its relaxed ears flicking forward as Lana called his name.

Vas turned away, looking for a spot to put Shiloh down. He settled on a small nook that was stacked high with equipment. With a long inhale, Vas swung Shiloh around into his arms before lowering him to the ground, leaning him against a saddle that rested on the floor. "You wanted to take a break, so here we are." He rubbed at his shoulder, rolling it back and testing its movement.

"This is Shiloh's horse," Lana said, and Lu pressed his nose against her back.

"That could be useful," Vas said. "Where are we even going in this city?"

Lana tossed a glance toward the horse and shrugged slightly, not wanting to answer.

"Right. Of course. You were just blindly following this unconscious guy around," Vas mumbled.

"I was not!" Lana's attention snapped back to Vas. Embarrassment made her uncomfortably hot. She had been blindly trusting Shiloh just because he'd saved her from the Hollows. Was she naïve? No. She could trust him. She had to.

"If you say so." Vas raked his fingers through his messy hair, being careful to untangle the knots that had formed around his horns.

Lana frowned at Vas, thoughts and memories bubbling to the surface. He reminded her, painfully, of Liam, which only steeled her resolve. Lana vowed to do everything she could to save their home from the Hollows so they could go back together, safe. Maybe she could even go to college with him once the Hollows were gone. The thought brought a flutter of hope.

Lu shifted forward, his ears pinned back as he huffed at Shiloh's unconscious form. Tendrils of purple smoke twisted from Lu's nostrils and his flesh quaked, shifting rapidly from black to purple smoke before solidifying again.

Vas watched the horse with narrowed eyes, and Lana watched Vas. "So, where are you actually from?" Vas asked her.

Lana smiled at the horse and ignored Vas's question. "Do you think Lu could help us navigate the city?"

"Maybe," Vas said. "Where are you from, Lana?"

Something about the way he asked felt intense. Did he somehow know she wasn't from Kaelum? How could he? Would it matter if he knew?

She walked over to the horse and held her hand hesitantly toward it. Lu lifted his head and huffed against her hand. Its eyes never left her face as it curiously breathed against her skin. She didn't flinch as it moved its lips, brushing them against her hand and feeling her fingers in that way horses do, rocking their lips back and forth and grabbing like little hands. She was surprised that its glassy flesh was cold, but not hard and inflexible.

"Are you not going to answer my question?" he asked as he leaned against the wooden wall.

"I don't really think it matters much." Lana shrugged as she dropped her hand from the horse's face.

"It matters to me."

"Why?" Lana walked away from where Lu stood, but he followed. His head stayed low, near her shoulder.

Lana leaned against the wall, mirroring Vas on the other side of the room, and Lu rested beside her.

"Because I need to know. I'm trapped down here with you, and—" Vas halted his sentence and let it fall flat. He glanced away, the intensity of his gaze softening.

"And what?"

"I want to know. I want to know you. You feel familiar."

She didn't admit it, but he felt familiar too. So, despite the logic saying she shouldn't trust a random fae she'd met, she decided to tell him the truth. "Well, there's no way we have met before. I've never come here except in my night-mares. Really, I'm not even sure that this isn't still just a nightmare." She bit her lip and looked over at the warm gaze of the horse, who seemed more discerning than any horse she'd ever met. His gaze was sharply curious, strange, and a bit unsettling. "Maybe I hope I'm dreaming—that would be simpler."

"You're not dreaming unless we both are." He flexed his fingers. "I don't understand what you mean, that you came here in your nightmares. I didn't think Havenites had magic like that—visions and projection—and dreamwalkers haven't made their way to Kaelum in centuries." He paused. "Are you not from Kaelum at all? Are you a dreamwalker?"

Lana shrugged. "I didn't think magic existed, so I have no clue about visions or dreamwalkers, or whatever. My mom, I think, she's from Haven, but where I'm from, there is no magic."

Vas froze. His eyes grew distant and his breath shallow. "When I was in the wellspring—"

Lu lifted his head suddenly, and his eyes went wild, searching up toward the ceiling. He pawed at the ground and nudged Lana's shoulder sternly.

She yelped and jumped away. "What? I thought you were nice."

Lu whinnied softly, almost a whisper, if horses could whisper. Then they all fell silent, straining their ears toward the ceiling, where an insistent scraping broke the silence. Something in the window caught Lana's eye. Shadowy shapes moved beyond the stained glass.

Lana backed into the horse and fought to breathe. Her heart hammered against her chest. They had found a way down. The Hollows were here.

Vas followed her gaze and swore under his breath when his eyes caught sight of the shifting shapes beyond the glass.

"What are we going to do?" Lana murmured.

"Get out of here, now." Vas groaned as he pulled the still unconscious Shiloh back onto his shoulders.

Lu carefully approached Vas and stared him down with his dark gaze.

"I think he wants to help," Lana said.

"Yeah, okay. Or lead us straight into the heart of the Hollows. I can't believe you're trusting a random magic horse you just met, even if it is Shiloh's horse." Vas rolled his eyes, but was already attempting to push Shiloh up onto Lu's back. The horse knelt slightly, allowing Vas to drape Shiloh across the horse's back.

"I guess that's kind of my MO right now. Random magic creatures are better than those things." She pointed out toward the writhing shadows that were still circling just beyond the stable.

"Why haven't they come in yet?" Vas stepped away from the horse and rubbed his shoulder. "Maybe it would be better to stay here."

Lu gave Vas a wild look and huffed.

"I think he knows more about this than we do."

"I hate this," Vas mumbled.

"Just come on." Lana reached out for Lu's mane. He dipped down again, closer to the ground than he had before, allowing Lana to pull herself up onto his enormous back. She struggled, but after a moment, settled herself just behind Shiloh.

Lu waited, tossing his head toward Vas.

He hesitated long enough to hear the chorus of howls that started up outside. A high-pitched screech that paled Vas's stony complexion cut through the noise for a moment.

Another roar from the same higher-pitched creature sent the Hollows in a frenzy. Suddenly Hollows were at the door, clawing at the walls and shattering the delicate stained windows. Lana stifled a scream as her heart jumped into her throat at the chaos descending upon them.

Vas jumped onto Lu's back; the horse shot up and then galloped down the hallway, breaking through the stable door. The doors slammed backward, knocking small dog-like Hollows flying. Lana tightened her fingers in Lu's mane and put her entire weight across Shiloh to keep him on the horse's back.

The small Hollows yelped as they rolled aside and some snapped at Lu's hooves, but he was too quick. His muscles moved together and made that same beautiful glass chiming as he leapt past the horde of Hollows. Vas's arms tightened around Lana, keeping her on the horse despite the maneuvering. At this moment, she was glad that her mother had insisted on riding lessons when she was young, though it had been years since she'd been on a horse.

Lana looked back toward the stable that was crawling with Hollows and saw one on the roof. The Hollow on the roof was tall and graceful, more human than the rest, delicate in a feminine way. Short, black hair moved wildly about her face, shifting with the cavern breeze, or perhaps the magic of the shadows that twisted around her. She was power personified, and it sent a shiver down Lana's spine as they escaped the undulating crowd of Hollows.

Lu galloped, putting more distance between them and the stable. The Hollows wouldn't be able to catch up, even if they were fast, and Lana knew they were, but Lu was faster.

CHAPTER 3

The Hollow Queen

The mage and his new friends had gotten away from her, but she didn't mind. The mage had never been a hindrance to her plans–in fact, his obsession with breaking the spell wall was entirely in her favor. Now, with the wall finally down, she wouldn't waste time thinking about whatever he was up to now. Even if he stood against her, they would fail.

Deep in the cave systems that ran underneath Haven, the Hollow Queen sat alone on her makeshift throne of cushions. Though alone, she never had peace or quiet in her mind. The voices of the pack were deafening. The anger, sorrow, grief, and unending hunger of every Hollow fought for her attention.

The queen longed to quiet the pack link, and had hated its overwhelming presence since she turned. Every emotion—all of it—ran down the thread of the pack bond to torment her. She ran her hand through her short, black hair, massaging her temples. *What was she missing?* The ancient Hollows couldn't have lived like this. They had a functioning court, a civilization. *How could they have lived with this pain?* Not to mention the stench on the feral Hollows was suffocating. And the hunger.

Her fangs ached and her stomach twisted at the thought of the unending hunger that only consuming magical energy could satisfy. She would need to journey to the wellspring soon to sate her thirst, but not yet. Her mind wandered back to her cursed existence. *Cursed.* The word throbbed in her mind. Were the Hollows a cursed fae? Was she cursed? Was the problem her? Would the Hollows be able to exist as they had in ancient times with a better ruler? The pain in her head spiked, piercing through her thoughts.

She doubled over for a moment, taking deep breaths, begging for the intensity to subside. How long had it been since she fed? How long had it been since she'd let the magic shift her body. She opened her mouth on a hiss, letting the magic explode from her body in a sheet of black shadow, taking some of the pain with it. In her pain, she almost let the magic consume her, to change her in hopes the pain would disappear, but she couldn't. It was too risky to shift like the other Hollows did.

Even though she ruled them, she had never given in completely to the beastly side beneath her skin— her Hollow form. When she shifted into that shadowy beast form, she only ever let the magic take hold of small parts of her, like elongating fingers and nails to deadly claws or lengthening her canines into true fangs, capable of rending flesh.

If she let herself bend completely to the magic, what would happen? Would the pack lose their madness? Or would she merely join them? The pack bond, so much like a mate bond. *Mate.* Her thoughts circled around the thin thread of her weak mate bond, though it still existed it was raw and painful to touch. Her mate had rejected her, their bond nearly broken — that was until the mage's spell that bound them together again. As much as the mage irritated her, she was grateful for him in that. A rejected bond was a broken, painful existence. *Was it so simple? Had she rejected the pack?* If that were the true cause, then the pain and madness might be soothed if she accepted them, but to accept the pack she would need to take the risk and shift. There was too much on the line for risks.

The Hollow queen squeezed her hands around her head, making a crown of her fingers, as she willed the ache of her existence to ease.

A giant piece of black glass hung beside her throne. Smoke twisted across the glass in a swirl of purple, the image of her advisor appeared. He bowed deeply. "My queen, do you need assistance? You seem troubled." He pushed his dark hair away from his eyes as he righted himself.

Troubled? He couldn't imagine how troubled she was, suffering in the den alone, yet surrounded by the Hollows' pain. Suddenly, her loneliness struck her. She was the queen of the most vicious army in Silvis. She would take the Silvid crown, become queen of the entire nation, but she was alone. Instinctively, she reached for her frayed mate bond, but she couldn't feel anything. Her heart ached, but she twisted her sorrow into anger. She had no use for tears in the world of Hollows.

"If anything, I'm troubled by all the soldiers I lost on your strange mission to the mundane world. The wolves may be the most common Hollow form, but they're also the best soldiers and I lost ten to that lunatic human." *Ten Hollows.* She forced her thoughts away. War was a necessity of conquest, and conquest a necessity if the Hollows were ever to have a peaceful future in Silvis as they had in the ancient past. She'd always known that, but it didn't stop the guilt from eating away at her. Ten lives lost.

"It is a regrettable loss, my queen, but the reward will certainly be worth it. The human entered Kaelum as a result of that attack." He bowed his head again.

"What's so special about that human, anyway?" She dropped her hands into her lap. She raised her head, staring at her advisor with a regal air.

"Is there nothing familiar about him to you? The green of his gaze, the shape of his face?"

The queen tapped her fingers on the arm of her throne of cushions, feeling impatient with her advisor's labyrinthine way of speaking. In the Silvid Court, nobility were always like this, so she should be used to it. She grimaced. She was sick of the wordplay of fae courts. "Why would I know a human from the mundane world? Say what you mean before I decide to feed you to the Hollows."

An amused smile tugged at the corner of the advisor's mouth. "Of course, my queen. I believe the boy is a changeling. I suspect that the fae soul residing in that human's body is one of the most powerful Silvids who ever lived. If we could bring him to our side, he would make a useful ally."

"I suppose a fae like that would be useful." She steepled her fingers below her chin. Once again, the advisor had proved his worth. "I trust you to handle this matter."

"With pleasure, my queen. The human is already in Haven. Now that the spell wall has finally broken, it will be easy to extract him when the time is right." He bowed deeply before his image wavered and disappeared from the black mirror.

The Hollow queen sat on her throne in the empty room, with only her heartache and ambition to keep her company.

CHAPTER 4

Lana

The horse didn't slow until they were deep in the city, after making so many twisting turns that Lana and Vas had no idea where they were or how to get back out again. After they were faraway from the Hollows, Lana and Vas had taken the time to move Shiloh, sitting him upright instead of hanging haphazardly. Shiloh's unconscious form leaned limply against Lana, and they'd used the ties from the bags to secure him. Vas's arm wrapped around them both to keep them steady. The constant warmth of his touch seared her skin. She felt overly conscious of every place he brushed against her. It was strange and she couldn't decide whether or not it was pleasant.

She barely knew him, which usually made her skin crawl at the thought of a stranger touching her. And yet he seemed so familiar—like someone she'd known all her life, someone she was bound to know in every life, someone her soul recognized. She felt silly to even think something so far-fetched, but then again, she was in a Faerie realm, riding a magic horse with an unconscious mage, so anything was possible, wasn't it? But, no. More likely was that Anastasia recognized him, had some sort of feelings for him. Lana took a deep breath, reminding herself that these strange feelings didn't belong to her, her feelings were for Liam. She shoved all her thoughts into the dark recesses of her mind.

Lana turned her gaze to the surrounding city. She thought Haven felt similar to the bigger cities from back home, only empty, but she'd only been to a bigger city once or twice. Then, she had been overwhelmed by the people. Now, it was the enormous buildings stretching toward the height of the cavern that felt like an oppressive, silent force.

The glowing moss had broken free of its lantern confines almost everywhere. It blanketed the sides of buildings and the sidewalks, casting an eerie blue glow from every direction. The horse walked carefully now that they were in the inner city. In the outer portion of the city, the buildings were much farther apart, with easily enough room for four lanes of traffic, though there seemed to be no technology Lana recognized. No cars. No carriages, even, just enormous stone buildings and empty roads.

As they entered what seemed to be the deepest parts of the city, the buildings squeezed together, like a historic downtown. She marveled at the place. It stirred some awe and desperate desire in her. She wondered what it looked like before, when it was full of people, bustling and doing.

She sighed. This wasn't a place for dreaming. She straightened herself, trying to focus on the reality of where they were—a foreign city, underground, where monsters stalked the shadows. Buildings around them were in more disarray here than anywhere else. On the outskirts and the first part of the city, the buildings had shown some wear with time, particularly where the moss was growing, but here, some buildings were completely collapsed.

Large slabs of stone scattered across the street, blocking paths and making the narrow streets even more narrow. Lu stepped up onto the sidewalk and pushed up close to a building, slipping through a small gap in the stone debris. Lana looked down as the toe of her shoe barely brushed against a patch of moss and came away with a dust of glow, almost like pollen. Vas carefully leaned down and brushed the dust from Lana's shoe, testing it in his fingers curiously. The powder was stubborn and clung to his fingers. He shoved his hand in his pocket, wiping his fingers off in the fabric there. When he pulled his hand back out, his fingers were free of the glowing dust.

On the other side of the narrow stone gap, the street opened into a large square. The cobblestone sidewalk joined up with several other side streets into a large plaza of mosaic stone. At the center was a fountain—an incredibly ornate fountain.

Lana gaped at the twisting sculpture, embedded with a shimmering glass of a multitude of colors. The horse stopped at the edge of the fountain and blew air through his nose.

"What?" Lana whispered. Her voice cracked, and she realized this was the first time she'd spoken in hours.

Lu twisted his head to look at her with one brown eye and huffed again. He moved to the back of the fountain, where the stone rim was much higher and larger, big enough that even Lu was easily hidden behind it. He scraped his hoof at the base of the stone.

Vas leaned toward the stone, inspecting it from where he still sat on Lu's back. A thin, straight crack ran across the design of the stone. He followed it with his fingers until it turned sharply down at a ninety-degree angle and dropped all the way in another thin, straight line until it met with the floor.

"This opens. It's a door," Vas said.

"Okay, but how do we open it?"

"Why does the horse want us to open it?" Vas asked.

Lu huffed impatiently and moved to the side of the fountain where he had initially stopped. He craned his neck, brown eyes landing on Shiloh's unconscious form. Lana patted Lu's shoulder and shifted to get down. The horse immediately bent down to help her reach the ground. Lana untied the knot that held Shiloh against her, and she carefully climbed down from the horse.

Vas furrowed his brow, holding Shiloh awkwardly now that Lana had dismounted. "Are we sure he's not dead?" Vas reached up and patted Shiloh's face. "Maybe I should take him down."

Lana shrugged. "Might as well." She inspected the rim of the fountain, pushing at the various designs around the ridge, hoping something would give and the door at the back would open.

Vas frowned and grabbed Shiloh's shoulders to keep him steady as he shifted his weight to dismount. Lu bent down again to facilitate the movement. "This horse is spookily well trained," Vas muttered. As his feet hit the ground, he clumsily pulled Shiloh into his arms, nearly falling and dropping him.

Lana rushed over to help until they were both steady again, but even after, she couldn't help but stare at them both. Vas sat Shiloh down against the edge of the fountain, leaning his back against the stone so he sat upright, and then kneeled in front of him.

In the brighter light of the plaza, black streaks became apparent near Shiloh's eyes and nose. Vas reached out and swiped his fingers along a streak near Shiloh's eye.

"Soot," he said and wiped his fingers on Shiloh's pants. Even the fringe of Shiloh's hair that framed his face was singed. Vas swore underneath his breath before taking a deep breath and looking up at Lana.

She'd been wasting time watching him. With a frown, she concentrated on the fountain. Shiloh was a mage, so surely this must be magic, right? If she could just remember what she felt back in the temple, that warm glow radiating off of Anastasia while she slept. Lana hovered her hand above the rippling water of the fountain and closed her eyes. She just needed to find that hint of golden warmth, like the sun at the end of summer, caressed by an early autumnal breeze.

A fading, flickering feeling caught her attention, and she shoved her entire hand into the fountain water. A wide grin stole across her face. At the bottom, a piece of stone shifted beneath her fingers. Finally, she'd found something that moved. She pressed her palm into the square of stone at the bottom of the fountain. A tiny golden glow, like the magic that had once surrounded Shiloh, danced across her fingertips. Its warmth raced up her arm, dancing and tingling, bringing a strange giddiness with it.

With a grinding pop, the door at the back of the fountain opened.

"Careful!" Vas jumped up and moved toward her.

"What?!" Lana jerked her hand from the water and the glow dissipated.

"Your hand was glowing."

Lana grinned. "I know! It's awesome!" But more than that, it felt like home, but surely that was because of Anastasia.

This wasn't her magic. It was her sister's. Her ecstasy fell away, leaving her feeling cold and out of place.

"No." Vas raked a hand through his hair quickly. "You don't know how to be careful with it. You said you're not from here. Where you're from, there is no magic, right?"

"Well, yeah." Lana walked around to the open door at the back of the fountain.

Vas pointed at Shiloh. "Magic happened to him."

"He fell down the stairs and was exhausted." Lana paused before continuing uncertainly. "Besides, I think he knows magic."

"His hair is singed, and he has soot on his face." Vas gestured down to Shiloh. "Magic is consuming. It's not something to be used without thought. Human magic is like sun and fire. That must be what happened to him."

"And if it is? What do we do?" She tried to keep the panic from her voice. What would she do if Shiloh never woke up?

Vas turned away, shifting his attention from Lana back to the crumbling city around them. "I don't know."

Fear and frustration twisted in her gut. "Super helpful." Lana stood in front of the door and looked down. The horse had brought them here for a reason. Maybe whatever Shiloh needed to wake up was down there. The path was well lit with torches of shimmering golden light. It led down and was wide and tall enough to even accommodate Lu. Lana stared down in awe.

Lu huffed at her hair and nudged her shoulder gently toward the staircase.

"All right," she said. "Let's go."

"I don't understand why you keep blindly following this horse."

"He's not just a horse. Have you seen him? He's magic. I think it's pretty clear that he's not trying to hurt us. In fact, he saved us from the Hollows, and he's Shiloh's horse."

"But now he's pushing us to go down an unknown corridor. Maybe he saved us from the Hollows so he could eat us."

Lu huffed and snapped at the air toward Vas.

"See!" Vas said.

"No. He just doesn't like you because you're ridiculous and rude. Grab Shi and come on." Lana paused. "Or don't. I don't know why you keep coming with me if you think I'm being reckless."

"Maybe I'm wondering that myself," Vas said. But despite that, he leaned down and pulled Shiloh up onto his back.

With Lana at the lead and Lu making up the rear, they all descended into the fountain staircase. The door slid shut behind them, leaving them closed off from the city with no way to go but forward.

A few flights down the stairs stopped, opening into a large room with electric lights buzzing in the ceiling. A tousled bed sat in one corner and in the opposite corner was a large mat, like a giant dog bed, and was even piled on one side with pillows and blankets, as if someone had slept there as well. There was a small kitchen area and a couch with a short table that sat in front of it, cluttered with books and papers.

Vas stepped past Lana and walked into the room, making a beeline for the bed, where he laid Shiloh down. Vas stretched and rubbed at his shoulder.

Lana moved to the center of the room, turning in a circle to look at everything. She was surprised by how much it looked like a studio apartment. The kitchen had a sink and a refrigerator. *Electricity?* The rest of the city glowed with mosslight. *How had he managed this?* She almost laughed, but stopped and her gaze landed on Lu. "Is this where Shiloh lives?"

Lu dropped his head and jerked it upward like a nod. The horse gingerly moved to Shiloh's side, pressing his muzzle against Shiloh's cheek. Purple smoke gathered around Lu, flowing from his nostrils with each breath.

"Well, all right then. Maybe there's something to help him around here."

"Or at least maybe some water." Vas went to the kitchen. He turned on the sink and clean water flowed from it. He leaned down and pressed his mouth into the stream.

"You could at least use a cup." Lana sat down on the couch and bent over the notes on the coffee table. It was all unintelligible to her. The words twisted together in familiar ways, but it was utterly foreign. "Can you read this?"

Vas, now with a cup of water in his hand, pulled a loaf of bread off the counter before joining Lana on the couch. He set a chunk of bread and the cup beside her. "Of course I can. You should eat or at least drink."

He sat, and she obeyed with little resistance. She gulped the water, only pausing to watch him rifle through the pages and books.

"So what's it say?" Lana asked.

"Good question." Vas turned another page over. "I can't read this."

"But you said you could?" Lana looked over at Shiloh. *Maybe she should give him some water. Or would he choke if she tried?* She frowned, wondering what to do.

"I don't know what language this is. It looks similar to the writings of the Silvids, but I don't know. There are some notes in the margins I can make out, but it makes no sense. I've never studied soul magic." Vas continued reading, holding the book close to his face, enthralled.

"Then we've got to look somewhere else." Lana stood, shoving the last bit of bread into her mouth to quench the hunger that sank its claws into her gut and wouldn't relent. Trying to ignore the strange void-like feeling inside her, she reasoned it must be anxiety and shoved the thoughts and feelings away.

Lana looked around again. A few bookshelves lined the walls. After a quick look, she realized most of the books were written in that same foreign language, but the few she could read seemed to just be fairy tales.

"If his condition results from magic use, then there's nothing we can do but wait." Vas snapped the book shut and placed it back on the table.

The horse stood by Shiloh's side, huffing at his face.

She turned her attention back to the books for a moment. There was nothing she could do. There was no one to help. The Hollows were probably out prowling the city by now. She couldn't save Feyville alone. Liam and her body were somewhere in this city. She needed Shiloh. He was the only one who knew the answers to her questions.

She dropped to the floor and buried her face in her hands. She was exhausted and scared.

"Lana!" Vas shouted. The coffee table scraped the floor as he pushed it away and jumped to his feet.

Lana lifted her head, scrambling up as well, certain the Hollows were closing in again. Instead, she saw Lu. A shifting cloud of purple-hued smoke obscured his body. When the smoke cleared, the horse was gone.

CHAPTER 5

Lana

In place of the glass-like horse stood a man with straight black hair that hung down to his chest. His fingers slipped across Shiloh's cheek. Ignoring Lana and Vas, the man went to the kitchen and filled a glass with water, which he immediately brought back to Shiloh's side.

He brushed the singed hair away from Shiloh's face before slipping a hand beneath his head. The man lifted Shiloh's head carefully and tipped some of the water into his mouth.

At the first touch of water, Shiloh's eyes fluttered. Even still asleep, he drank heavily. His fingers twitched, as if desperate to clasp onto the cup. He pulled the cup away from Shiloh's face and set it aside.

"He nearly did it this time," he murmured with a sigh. His fingers moved across Shiloh's face, gently wiping the smut from around his eyes and nose. Finally, the man turned to Lana and Vas. "How long has he been unconscious?"

She had been trusting the horse the entire time. Did it make any difference that the horse was also a man? No. In fact, this was for the best. He would know how to help Shiloh, so for now she would answer whatever questions he had. Lana tilted her head up in thought, staring at the ceiling as if the sight would help her recall the countless hours. "I don't know," she finally said. "We escaped the Hollows in the temple and then when we got to the bottom of the stairs, he just fainted."

His brows shot up. "He fell unconscious on the stairs? That's at least a day's journey." He turned back to Shiloh, pulling up on his eyelids to look into his unseeing eyes. Still not satisfied, he grabbed Shiloh's jaw and pulled his mouth open, peering inside. After a long moment, he finally let Shiloh go. His shoulder relaxed as he turned back to Lana and Vas.

Silence stretched across the room for a long moment.

"Why did you not reveal yourself sooner?" Lana asked.

The man's gaze was firmly on Vas, his brows furrowing in deep contemplation. He blinked a few times, as if coming out of deep thoughts. "Reveal? Oh, you mean the horse? I'm not skilled in shifting, though it is a talent of my family. Once I've shifted, it takes much too long to regain the strength to shift again. Would you have rather walked the length of the city?"

"I suppose not," Lana said.

The man had a long face and wore an amused expression, though his slight smile didn't reach his eyes, which continued to dart between Lana and Shiloh's unconscious form. He straightened his clothes—a simple button-down shirt, deep purple, carefully tucked into dark denim jeans.

"I'm glad you remembered my name—though only Shiloh calls me Lu," the man said, forcing a smile. "Though there is something quite different about you, Anastasia. I suppose Shiloh was finally successful, though he is in a dreadful state now."

"I'm not Anastasia."

Lu lifted a dark brow. "Is that so? I had thought it weird this Brynian pup was calling you such an odd name." He smiled and rolled her name across his tongue. "Lana. Cute."

"Pup?!" Vas sneered.

"Well, you didn't recognize one of your own. So either you are young or just foolish." The man inspected Vas carefully. "My name is Luze. Don't I know you?"

"Wait," Lana said. "What do you mean? One of your own?"

The corner of Luze's lip lifted into a half smile, and his eyes softened as he looked toward Lana. "I'm Brynian as well."

"But," Lana looked at Shiloh's sleeping form, "he said I shouldn't trust Vas because he was Brynian. But...you?"

Luze narrowed his eyes, staring at Shiloh for a moment before letting his expression smooth back into amused friendliness. "I suppose I'm a bit different. Humans love a fae turned traitor." Luze sighed. "Shiloh and I met during the first battles of the war. Your young ram here likely doesn't remember the war. Now it's not much of a war, since the Hollows have been trapped in the desert."

"I remember it," Vas interrupted. His brows furrowed in confusion. "It's not like it was that long ago."

Luze ran his eyes over Vas again, considering his statement, and then shrugged. "I didn't entirely agree with the ideals of our king. He's a good man, but unrealistic. A daydreamer. I certainly didn't trust his advisor, so not long before the wall went up, I made myself useful here, with the humans. Though, I sometimes wonder if I could have somehow prevented the queen's death."

"I'm incredibly confused." Lana looked toward Vas, hoping he could illuminate something, but he was frozen.

Vas's eyes were wide, searching Luze's face. "You mean the Brynian king in Brynia, right? And the Brynian queen?"

Luze scrunched up his face. "What? No. I mean the Silvid queen's consort. The supposed king of this land."

"No. I don't understand." Vas stepped backward, nearly tripping over a stack of books on the floor.

Lana turned instinctively, reaching for Vas's arm to steady him. "What's wrong?"

Confusion fogged Luze's face. "You didn't know?"

Lana looked back at Luze for a moment. "What do you mean? Didn't know what?"

Vas slouched to the floor and stared off into space.

"The Silvid queen was much beloved. Before her death, there were only skirmishes of Hollows. The nobles certainly called it a war, but the war didn't truly begin until her death."

Lana kept her hand on Vas's shoulder, but he was unresponsive. After a moment, he buried his face against his knees, which were pulled up against him as he sat on the floor.

"He must have been living under a rock for the last twenty-five years," Luze said.

Once again, silence descended upon the small apartment. Lana shifted awkwardly. She didn't know what to do. Vas's pain was so obvious, it was as if she could feel his grief herself. The weight of it choked her, but what could she do? She barely knew him.

She chewed on her bottom lip and then sank down on the couch near Vas. There was nothing she could do but look for answers, so she cleared her throat. Talking to Luze would surely give her more answers than digging through Shiloh's apartment. "What were you checking for?" she asked.

Luze pushed Shiloh's legs over and sat at the edge of the bed. His eyes never left the slow rise and fall of Shiloh's chest, as if he would stop breathing if he looked away. "To see if he would ever wake up."

"And will he?" Her fingers tightened instinctively on Vas's shoulder. *What would she do if Shiloh didn't wake?*

"Most probably." Luze clasped his fidgeting hands together in his lap.

Lana forced herself to relax, releasing her grip on Vas, who still sat with his face buried against his knees. She wanted to comfort him, though she had no idea why a queen's death had upset him so much, so she left her hand relaxed against his shoulder. Turning her attention back to Luze, she asked, "How do you know he will wake up?"

Luze paused, considering her question. "Humans are a bit of odd ones when it comes to magic. Magic is wild. Too much can fundamentally change a fae, cause them to go mad in some ways or even alter their genetic makeup entirely, but humans aren't built to withstand magic. Too much and they burn from the inside out." He frowned.

"I don't understand. How do you tell?"

Never taking his eyes from Shiloh, Luze scratched at his chin with a trembling hand. "Well, his eyes still look like eyes and not ash. His mouth and tongue are still pink, not black. I'd say he still has all the signs and symptoms of being alive, and not of being a breathing husk, so there you go."

Luze wrapped his hand around Shiloh's wrist, pressing two fingers at the base of his thumb. After a long moment passed, he picked up Shiloh's hand and placed it delicately against Shiloh's chest. In a slow, deliberate motion, Luze stood up.

Vas was still motionless, with his arms wrapped around his knees, pulling himself as tight as he could.

"I would like to know what happened before you found the stable." Luze narrowed his eyes at Lana, letting his gaze drift back and forth between the pair on the floor.

Lana shifted, putting herself slightly between Vas and Luze, who smiled. The gesture settled across his body and relaxed his posture; he tossed his hair back away from his face.

"But I suppose that story can wait. I have other things to tend to, anyway." In a few strides, Luze was back in the kitchen. He slid open a door that, until now, had seemed to be just another part of the wall.

"Thank you," Lana said, just as the door slid shut. She then turned her attention to Vas. She had no idea what to do or say or even what was wrong. "Vas?"

He didn't move or speak.

"Luze left. Shiloh's still unconscious. It's just you and me."

He still didn't respond.

"You wanted to know where I'm from. I could tell you about it, if you wanted to know."

Her words were met with more silence.

"Or if there was something else. Some other thing you were curious about. I could—"

"Lana." He interrupted her. His voice was barely a whisper. He lifted his face so that only his eyes, heavy with tears, peered from the safety of his arms. "I just would like some time to process this."

"Oh." She stared at his red-rimmed eyes. "Um. Okay. Sure." She pushed herself up from the couch. "Just let me know if you want to talk or something."

He continued to stare up at her, as if searching her face for the answers that he didn't have, but she didn't have any answers for him either. "Thank you," he said. "For your failed attempts at distraction. I want nothing right now."

"If you ever want something, I've been told that talking can help sometimes," she said, feeling hypocritical that she never took her own advice. "Sleep might help too. The couch is right there." She offered him a slight smile. "I'll be over here."

Vas pushed himself off the floor and climbed over to the couch, where he collapsed face-first.

Soon after, Lana busied herself by snooping around the room. Vas was sound asleep. She knew they had been traveling and running from the Hollows for quite a while now, but somehow she didn't feel tired. She was buzzing with energy that begged to escape.

She paced the floor, realizing she was alone now in this room with two unconscious strangers. More than that, she was inside a stranger. This wasn't even her body. In fact, she didn't even know where her body was. When Shiloh came to, she would need to talk to him about where Liam and her body were. Maybe Luze had known. She frowned and pressed her hand against the wall, where Luze had disappeared. If she could figure out how to open it, she could find Luze and ask him where Liam was.

She tried to pry open the door, tried pushing and pressing everything she could find, but nothing happened. *Had Luze used some kind of magic?* She groaned and slammed her fist against the closed door. Trapped and frustrated, she just wanted to be with Liam again. If she could just see him, she would feel better.

Liam. With just the thought of him, all the buzz and energy slipped away from her, and Lana slumped down in a nearby chair.

She ran through the situation in her head. She was stuck in this place with no idea where Liam or her mother could be or how to figure it out. The guy who could help her was unconscious.

Then there was Vas. Lana glanced over at his sleeping form. He'd rolled over in his sleep and now faced her. His hair curled over his forehead, framing his peaceful expression. The sound of his breath was a calming rhythm, moving sweetly through his barely parted lips. She imagined brushing her fingers along his cheek, feeling the dichotomy between smooth skin and the roughness of his patchy stubble. Vas felt familiar and comfortable.

Lana desperately wanted to go home, but a part of her wished he could come with her. She thought Liam would like him, or maybe they'd hate each other. She couldn't always tell with Liam. He was a conundrum most days—or perhaps, Lana thought, she was just too oblivious to notice the nuances of him. She wished she had paid more attention when he was still around.

Or maybe she should have gone with him to college. Even if she hadn't enrolled in school, she should have gone. He'd asked her to go with him when he first left. Twice now in her life, he'd asked her to move in with him. He was always so worried, especially after Mom left. When he offered the first time, she had been tempted, but she hadn't. She couldn't even remember why she'd turned him down. Lana scoffed at herself. Fear probably. It had been his idea, not hers. She'd had no reason not to go. Now, she was trapped in the world of her nightmares.

This didn't feel like a nightmare, though. Lana frowned and flexed her fingers in front of her. Maybe real life was a dream. She buried her face in her hands. There was no use in falling into philosophical holes. Right now, this was her reality, and she needed to figure out what to do and how to get everyone home safely.

Lana dug her nails into her skin, focusing on the pain to clear her head. Thinking about everything was a hopeless endeavor. Instead, Lana decided she would snoop about the room some more. At the very least, she hoped to find a map. Understanding the layout of this place would bring some comfort, at least.

She sat down in front of the couch and dug through piles of notes that made no sense to her. She scattered books across the floor until her head throbbed from the mental effort.

"Hello," said a small voice.

Lana froze. She shifted up onto her knees and pushed away the coffee table full of papers. Better to defend herself if something came through the door.

"L-ana?" the voice called out again.

Lana held her breath. "Who are you?" she whispered, searching the room for the source of the strange voice.

"Finally. You can hear me," the voice murmured in relief.

"What do you mean? Who are you?"

Laughter bubbled up, growing stronger. *"Anastasia."*

"You're in my head," Lana said, as realization dawned on her. She sank back down to the floor, letting her back rest against the couch.

"Clever, aren't you," Anastasia teased.

"So, are you awake? We don't need to find the amulet, like Shiloh said?" Hope blossomed. If Anastasia was awake, then when Shiloh woke, he could help her go back to her own body and Anastasia could deal with the Hollows.

"I don't know—there's something wrong." Anastasia's voice wavered, fading in and out like a fuzzy radio station. *"I am broken into pieces."*

"What do I do?"

"Find Mom. She'll fix us," Anastasia whispered.

"I want to help you. You're my only sister. But how do I do that? How do I find her?"

"It hurts..." Her voice faded, taking the golden presence of her sister with it.

Lana's heart thundered in her chest and she turned her mind inward, desperately searching for Anastasia in the recesses of her thoughts. Lana shuddered as pain fractured through her, sizzling hot and wild.

She slumped against the couch until the fire consumed her. *Help us. Help them. Help me.*

CHAPTER 6

Vas

When Vas woke, he was alone. Lana had fallen asleep, slumped on the floor, her knees pulled up tight to her chest and her arms wrapped around them. She must have been exhausted to fall asleep like that.

He crouched beside her, peering at her face. How could she look so much like Anastasia? Was he misremembering the girl he'd only met once, only danced with one night? But, he never got her out of his head. From the moment he met her, she consumed his waking thoughts. Her face haunted his dreams. He wouldn't misremember her. The only difference he could see in Lana was her eyes — dark and warm like rain-damp soil. Could they be twins?

Lana had said it was complicated, and she grew up in the mundane world, where all humans had once lived. Had some strange magic separated them at birth? No. That was ridiculous. Why was he even bothering to contemplate it? She would tell him eventually. What he should ask instead, the question that tightened his heart with fear, was where Anastasia was now.

Lana groaned in her sleep, shifting until her body fell, unraveling the tight ball she'd been slumped in. Vas reached out, catching her before her head could hit to hard floor. The touch of her skin against his was an unexpected comfort. He knew he should let her go, but he didn't want to.

He slid his arms underneath her, steeling his resolve as he scooped her up and hurried her to the couch. He yanked his hands away from her, feeling guilty for touching her, even innocently, while she slept.

She's not Anastasia, he reminded himself. He'd only ever had feelings like this for Anastasia — those desires to stay by her side, to hold her close to him, wrap his arms around her and breathe in the earthy scent of her. Lana was not her, but his heart ached when he saw her smile, the arch of her brow, or heard her voice. Lana was a near perfect replica of Anastasia, who he now realized he missed fiercely even though they'd only met once. Could Lana really, truly be his mate? He thought back to that feeling by the stairs of Haven. The pull. It was unmistakable, but so much like what he'd felt with Anastasia. What was wrong with him?

He frowned down at Lana, who was now breathing deeply, and stepped away. In this quiet, he could barely stand to be near her. Where was Anastasia? He paced around the room, forcing his thoughts anywhere but on the past.

Time slipped past him, but Vas had no idea how long he'd been pacing, trapped in his spiraling thoughts. He laced and unlaced his fingers together as he paced, stalking around the room like a caged panther.

The bed was empty. Vas could only assume that Shiloh had woken and was completely fine somewhere. Not even Luze lurked in the corners. He had a strange nagging feeling about that fae, but he couldn't place it. The name felt familiar, but it was a common enough name; even one of his father's servants had been named Luze. *His father.* Vas shoved his fingers into his hair and massaged his aching head. *What had happened while he was trapped in the wellspring?*

Vas took a deep breath and halted his pacing. It was only making him feel worse, more crazed, trapped by this room, where—other than Lana, fast asleep—he was completely alone. He didn't know whether he preferred that, preferred being alone with his grief. *Grief? No.* He wouldn't accept it. His mother wasn't dead. There must be some misunderstanding. *How long had he been in the wellspring?* All the information that had been thrown at him since he found Lana swirled around in his head, threatening to explode.

The walls caged him. He couldn't leave for fear of the monsters that lurked in the city. Even if he left, he'd never find his way back out of the city. Though he knew he couldn't have escaped the desert alone either, he almost wished he had stayed out in the sunshine. The dark, broken corridors of the city were even less inviting than the shifting and bloodstained sands.

But then there was Lana. He sighed, frustration and confusion strangling his breath, and looked at her. He felt tied to her. The thought of leaving her side twisted his insides together and left him feeling nauseous and empty. Kneeling by the couch, he stared at her face again, frustrated by this feeling he didn't understand. A feeling so much like when he'd met Anastasia. But he couldn't have two mates, could he? He'd heard from his mother that some fae had multiple fated mates and some pairings were friendships, but this didn't feel like that.

But what haunted him most wasn't just her similarity to Anastasia. In her face, he saw the face of another. Her eyes were too much like the woman in his wellspring dreams. He sank back onto his heels at the sudden shift of his mind. He thought the effects of the wellspring had left him for good, but now he was being pulled back into memories of that other world, where he had lived as someone else.

The smell of coffee rose strongly in his nose, and he tried to rub it away. He blinked and a scene unfolded. He was sitting at a little cafe with a slender girl, who smiled at him with deep familiarity and love. His heart fluttered, but he knew he shouldn't feel this way about her. This girl was his friend. Not only that, he was leaving, but that didn't mean he had to leave her, did it? Hope blossomed in his chest.

He reached across the table and placed his hand on top of hers, squeezing it gently. The smile fell from her face. Their eyes met. Her deep-brown eyes were easy to fall into.

"I'm sorry," Vas said, though his voice wasn't his own. He pulled his hand away and pushed his glasses up on his nose.

"What? What's wrong?" Her face had paled.

"I meant to tell you sooner, but I thought we'd have more time before..." He trailed off. "I got accepted, and I'm moving to campus next weekend."

"Next weekend?" She pulled her hands into her lap and stared down at the table, hurt.

He knew her expressions better than his own.

"Next weekend," he confirmed. He couldn't stand seeing her like this. His heart leaped to his throat, and, fueled by that fluttering hope, he spoke before he could stop himself. "Come with me."

Her head jerked up, and her eyes caught his in surprise. "You want me to come with you?"

His throat was tight, so he nodded, afraid he'd betray his nervousness in his voice. He wiped his sweaty palms on his jeans.

She smiled, though her lips wavered. "I can't." She looked back down at her lap. "It'd be great to be roommates. You know I've always wanted to move away from here, but I just can't. I doubt my car could make it that far. I would need to find a job up there. It would just—I can't. Mom has been acting so weird lately. I can't leave her."

"Right. It was silly for me to ask." He laughed, though the sound fell flat. In his heart, he knew she wouldn't say yes, but maybe if he asked her again, she'd say yes one day. "You can always change your mind."

She smiled, still keeping her head bowed toward her lap. "Promise?"

He reached his hand across the table toward her, palm up, and his pinky finger stretched toward her. "Promise."

She looked up at him and then grabbed his pinky finger with hers, sealing the promise in the way they always had.

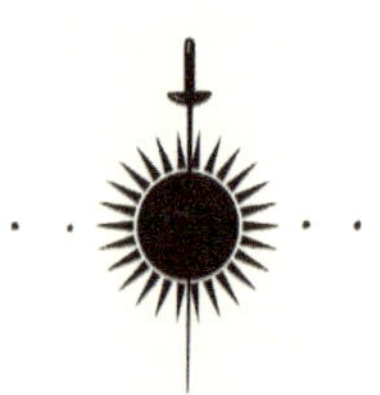

Vas fell back away from the couch, where Lana still slept. Golden magic lingered in the air between them, like mist. The mist faded, barely outlining the shapes of the cafe.

"Well, isn't that interesting," Shiloh said. He and Luze stood at the door, watching him.

Luze stepped forward to Vas's side and caught his face in his hand. He narrowed his eyes as he inspected his face. Their eyes met.

After a moment, Luze whispered, "I knew it."

"I didn't mean to." Vas frowned. "I don't know what happened. I was just sitting here with her and then..."

Luze's expression relaxed, and he dropped his hand from Vas's face.

"What were you thinking, then? Before you forced magic upon her and violated her memories?" Shiloh crossed his arms.

"I don't think this is necessary," Luze said. "He obviously lacks training, which I can provide, if you feel threatened by this child."

"I'm not a child." Vas frowned.

"What harm could he come to by answering me?" Shiloh smiled at Luze. "Tell me," he said to Vas.

Vas hesitated. Luze's body had tensed, and now Vas glared at Shiloh. "I just was thinking about leaving."

"I wouldn't stop you if you did." Shiloh gestured to the door beside him.

Vas clenched his fists and yanked his head up. "I won't leave her. I can't leave her." *Again*, said a little voice in the back of his mind.

Shiloh kept his eyes on Vas, scrutinizing him.

Vas could almost see the gears of Shiloh's mind turning and twisting. He didn't trust Shiloh. There was something fierce just beneath the surface of his gentle face.

After a long moment, Shiloh's lips twitched up into a slight smile. He crossed the room in only a few strides and pushed open the hidden door that led to the few other rooms in the house. He glanced expectantly toward them both, but Luze waved him on.

"I need something to eat, then I'll join you in the viewing room momentarily. I doubt there will be anything of interest yet," Luze sighed as he made his way to the kitchen.

Shiloh disappeared through the door and down the hallway, leaving Vas alone with Luze.

"I know what memory magic looks like," Luze said softly as he filled a glass of water. "That wasn't it. Gold is the magic of flame and the soul. Purple is Brynian magic of illusions and dreams, which I'm sure you well know, Prince." He opened the cabinet and dug around, retrieving a bag filled with dried fruit.

Vas stayed on the floor by Lana. He clasped his hands in front of him and didn't say a word, but his thoughts raced. *Prince.* He knew. *Did that matter? Would they force him to leave because of whatever political changes that happened while he was in the wellspring?*

"Have you even eaten anything lately?" Luze glanced over his shoulder toward Vas, who shrugged.

Luze grabbed another glass and filled it with something thick and sweet from the refrigerator. He walked over to Vas and set the glass down on the floor beside him. After grabbing a handful of dried fruit from the bag, he dropped it beside Vas.

"You know, I worked in the queen's court for..." he shrugged, "I don't know, almost my entire life."

Vas lifted the glass to his lips and took a small sip before replacing it on the ground. He stole a glance at Luze for just a moment before sinking further down on the floor, pulling his knees up to his chest. *Was he the servant he remembered?* But his father's servant had been about the same age as Vas—in his twenties—but this Luze seemed closer to his parents' age. It couldn't be the same fae, unless... The same question resurfaced, echoing through his mind: *How long had he been in the wellspring?*

"It's okay if you don't remember me," Luze said softly with a smile. "The king always said I was as silent as a shadow." His gaze drifted off, staring at the wall with a far-off expression.

Vas didn't speak. He didn't know what to say when his current reality made no sense.

Luze turned his attention back to Vas with a slight frown. "I'm sorry about your mother. If I had realized then, I would have been more gentle with my words."

Vas remained silent, resting his chin on his knees as he searched Luze's face, beginning to recognize the familiarity of his features. He really did look like his father's servant. If that were true, then he'd been in the wellspring for at least twenty years. *How was he still alive?* "What happened?" Vas asked, his eyes downcast.

Luze sat on the floor beside Vas in a swift, graceful movement. "Athanasios was...I don't know exactly, but after you...after we thought you were lost to the wellspring...he convinced the king to lead so many reckless experiments to rescue you. When the spell wall went up, the king was forced to give up. No more soldiers could enter the desert and nothing could escape it. Then your mother—well, we lost her to the Hollows. I left the Silvid Court before we lost the queen, so I'm not sure of the details. I've been gathering information for decades now through the magic mirrors. The onslaught of the Hollows needs to end. The king has disappeared, and now Athanasios..."

"What does Athan have to do with anything?" What had his family suffered in his absence? Grief hit Vas hard in the chest. If he hadn't been so reckless, would his mother have survived? Would his father have gone missing? Athan was the only person other than his father who truly admired his curiosity and encouraged him to learn and grow — to be something more than just the hated prince. "Did something happen to Athan?" Vas asked, panic seeping in. His family was in tatters. If something had happened to Athan, then Vas was truly alone in the world.

Luze furrowed his brows slightly and moved away, heading toward the hidden door that Shiloh had entered through minutes earlier. "I'm afraid if Shiloh is correct, you'll have the answer to that soon."

Luze stood and pushed through the hidden door, disappearing down the hallway.

"Wait!" Vas rushed after him. "What are you talking about?" He stepped into the hallway, leaving Lana alone and unconscious in the room. He hesitated for a moment, glancing back at her, before rushing after Luze.

Luze was already at the door at the far end of the hall, and didn't wait for Vas as he slipped inside. Ignoring the other doors in the hallway, Vas made his way to the end of the hall and pushed open the door without hesitation.

"Welcome to the viewing room." Luze stood a few paces away from the door, gesturing to the surrounding room. Three of the four walls were covered floor to ceiling with windows that looked out onto the plaza. Two recliners sat on one side of the room, facing the windows, but otherwise the room was completely empty. Magic symbols, pulsing with the purple energy of Brynian magic, covered the floor and climbed the walls like ivy. Shiloh looked up from where he leaned on the chair closest to the windows.

"I thought we were underground," Vas said. "Well... More underground than Haven already is."

"That's because we are." Shiloh rolled his eyes and shifted his gaze to Luze. "You were incorrect to assume that nothing interesting would happen yet." Shiloh gestured to the plaza, where Hollows were gathering.

Most of the creatures in the plaza were far from humanoid, looking like wolves and spiders and all sorts of beasts, but with grotesque mimicries of fae faces. Vas hadn't realized so many different types of Hollows existed. He grimaced with disgust as he looked at the nightmare creatures.

However, on nearby rooftops, a few Hollows more humanoid than the rest had assembled. These could have passed for Silvids if not for the red, pulsing vines that embedded in their skin like veins, twisting around their arms and legs and branching across their faces, and the shadowy magic smoke that clung to their bodies, swirling at their feet and resting there like a well-trained dog.

"I'm still hesitant to say you're right, Shiloh, but I suppose that is evidence of it." Luze stared intensely at the more Silvid-like Hollows.

"Can they see us?" Vas approached a nearby window, reaching his hand out to touch it.

Shiloh sighed. "Don't touch. And no. Of course not."

"Magic," Luze interjected with a smile. "What you see is the reflection of what is currently happening above us in the plaza, but those aren't windows. It's just glass and magic. Beyond the glass, just stone and dirt."

"The magic mirror spell." Vas brushed his fingers across the glass, despite Shiloh's command. The image rippled at his touch, distorting the vision of the plaza with small waves, like a pond. Athan had taught him this spell, one of the most difficult spells that Vas had learned during his brief and secretive magic lessons. "I didn't realize you could make such a large one. How are you sustaining it?"

Luze grinned. "I'm surprised you know of the spell. This one is an enchantment. Objects can hold spells and drain magic from the environment without a mage's influence as long as there is a wellspring nearby."

Vas marveled at the information—another sort of magic he'd never gotten the chance to study—before stepping away to the back of the room, where he observed the Hollows out in the plaza.

Shiloh, ignoring the interruption as if Vas didn't exist, picked up his conversation with Luze. "You're often hesitant to admit I'm right when you're clearly wrong."

"I don't doubt you about Athan, in theory. It's in practice that I'm uncertain. I don't think he's capable of having anything to do with this." Luze gestured at the group of Hollows. "Not that he wouldn't attempt to do something like this, but he simply can't. It's impossible. Hollows can't be commanded by magic, can't be created—they are born. You've read the same books that I have. I don't understand the basis for your theories, Shi."

"Athan is the strongest magician I have ever seen." Shiloh didn't turn away from the scene before him in the plaza.

"There's no other explanation for the Hollows on the mainland of Silvis. The wellspring is cut off from the mainland by the spell wall—or was. How else could Hollows exist outside of the desert if someone wasn't creating them somehow?"

"He's not capable of it. There's not a spell in existence that could do something like that," Luze said. "Besides that, Athan was trapped in the desert, too. He couldn't be creating Hollows on the mainland."

Shiloh growled in frustration. "Obviously, he must have contacted someone beyond the wall and channeled magic through them somehow."

"Do you not hear how ridiculous you sound, Shi?" Luze said, raising his brows with a smirk. "Who would Athan even be in contact with that could channel his magic?"

"Theoden," Shiloh said, crossing his arms as if he'd won the debate.

Vas flinched at the sound of his father's name. The taloned fingers of sorrow and guilt dug into his heart, squeezing painfully. He had been a reckless idiot and now it was too late.

"Just look at them!" Shiloh pointed at the humanoid Hollows. "They aren't like the rest. You've seen Athan with them!" Shiloh clenched his hands, taking up a fistful of fabric from his pants.

"I *think* I've seen him," Luze corrected. "And I think you're jumping to conclusions too quickly. The Silvids have fought against the Hollows since the Dae Era. Don't you think that if controlling them was within the realm of magic, they would have found out by now?"

Shiloh let out an exasperated breath. "Of course not! The Silvids barely use magic anymore. Only a select few can even admit to being able to use it. Magic is too feared and hated in Silvis for experimentation."

"All the more reason to know its limitations," Luze replied.

"Fear is the greatest keeper of ignorance."

They fell silent. Shiloh sat down in the chair rigidly and kept his eyes on the congregating Hollows. Luze ran his hand across his jaw. He held it there for a long moment before dropping his hand down to his side and stalking toward the door.

Luze opened his mouth to speak, but just pursed his lips together again before heading out of the door and down the hallway.

Vas looked at the back of Shiloh's head. The room felt smaller now that it was only the two of them. He crossed his arms and paced slowly back and forth across the room. "What are you accusing the Brynian king's advisor of doing?"

Shiloh spared a quick glance toward Vas. "Playing puppet master to the monsters."

"Why would he do that?"

"I'm sure he has plenty of reasons to, but doesn't it make perfect sense? The Brynian king consort desiring to return to the throne, despite the hostility of the people he wishes to rule over? The Silvids would never allow him the throne now that the true queen of Silvis has passed. So now what must he do? Take Silvis by force, and what better army than the beasts that the Silvids could never defeat?"

"No. It doesn't make sense. He wouldn't do that."

Shiloh smiled, watching Vas out of the corner of his eye. "Oh really? I think he would. He is the hated beast king for a reason. But either way, Luze has seen the king's experiments in the mirrors. After the queen passed, he kept a dungeon of Hollows and each day, he took one and chained it to laboratory tables."

"He would never do something like that, even to those horrid beasts." Vas curled his lips into a disbelieving sneer.

"Perhaps you should ask Luze yourself, then."

Vas scoffed and continued to pace, resigning himself to ignoring Shiloh.

CHAPTER 7

Lana

*F*lickering images filled her mind —

A twirling skirt of red and gold and an enormous ballroom. A man with bright green eyes laughed as she spoke, but it was all a blur. His face hid in the shadows. Then the image vanished, and another scene appeared.

Swords clashing and the familiar smile of a close friend. Alixandra.

"I don't know what you mean, Alix," Anastasia said as her blade slid along Alix's during their morning training. "You can't possibly mean that you'll kill Meredith."

"She's a traitor. What else can I do?"

Anastasia rolled her eyes. "So this is about the knighthood? The rules?"

Alix sung her sword down in a brutal chop, but Anastasia spun out of the way and circled behind Alix.

"No," Alix said. She whirled around, parrying Anastasia's blow with ease. "Mere ran off with the Hollows. She's with them now. Meredith chose them. She..." Alix faltered. Her words trailed off and a far-off look stole over her.

Anastasia hesitated with a frown, uncertain what to do when it was so clear her friend was suffering. "There must be something we're missing."

Alix shook her head and, in two quick steps, had her blade against Anastasia's neck. "I win." Without another word, Alix dropped her sword into her sheath and stalked off, leaving Anastasia dazed. The image faded again, giving way to another.

Wind howled through the nighttime desert, nearly overtaking the sound of screeching Hollows. Their scent brought bile to the back of Anastasia's throat, but she must continue.

If their mission tonight was successful, they would be a step closer to finding a solution—something that would end the Hollow war for good.

Something had excited the Hollows and brought them all to the wellspring, but she didn't have time to investigate. They needed to capture a Hollow for the mages to study. They hoped to find a way to defeat them once and for all. Alix, Shiloh, and Anastasia crouched behind a dune, watching the undulating pack with only a few of Haven's knights crouching behind them.

Shiloh pursed his lips, looking at Alix. "How are we supposed to separate just one? I wasn't expecting this." They had planned on stealth, but a horde this size would find them before they even got close enough to trap one of the smaller Hollows.

Alix pulled on her fingers, popping the knuckles one-by-one. After a long moment, she took a deep breath and pushed up from their hiding spot. She drew her sword and gave a meaningful look at Anastasia before plunging into the night.

They had done this before. Separate and kill. Tonight would be a slaughter. Anastasia grinned. She was ready. She jumped up and yanked her own blade from its sheath, and rushed forward. Tonight she would revel in being the Keeper of the Light. Her sword blazed suddenly with golden fire and the Hollows shrieked at their approach.

Anastasia caught up with Alix, who gave her a sidelong glance before holding her blade off to the side in front of her. A nervous, giddy laugh escaped Anastasia's lips as she caught Alix's blade with her own. The fire jumped from blade to blade.

Alix winced at the brightness of her sword and the two split ways, heading to either side of the mob of Hollows that were erupting around the wellspring. With the golden light, they cut through the Hollows. Their bodies erupted and quickly smoldered into ash with each fiery swipe of the Keeper's fire.

The Haven knights joined as well. They held their own against the Hollows, but it took several to down a beast without the fire. Even after death, the vines that clung to their bodies writhed on the ground and burrowed into the sand.

Alix and Anastasia culled the crowd until one Hollow, unlike the rest, stepped before them. Alix froze. The Hollow had a fae-like form, like a woman. Her short black hair dripped in shadows covering her face. Claws and shadowy fur climbed up her arms and across her chest, but Anastasia knew this fae. Anastasia's memories clouded and her head throbbed.

With a screech more horrible than she had ever heard, the beast called out to the others, who shrank away and retreated into the desert. Anastasia tossed a look towards Alix. They shared a wide-eyed horror. This Hollow held sway over the others.

Alix and Anastasia circled the Hollow. "Shiloh!" Alix called. "We have to capture her. I need her."

He nodded and moved into position with trembling hands. Alix thrust her sword, still ablaze with Anastasia's molten magic, swiping towards the Hollow. The Hollow didn't move, letting the blade sink into her stomach.

She didn't even flinch as the same fiery magic poured from Shiloh's outstretched hands. Anastasia lunged at the Hollow, but she wasn't quick enough.

The Hollow twisted, pulling Alix's blade from her hand, and grasped Anastasia's sword in her claw. She ripped both of the swords away and threw them aside with unnatural strength.

Red blood poured from the Hollow's wound, startling Anastasia. This was different. Hollow blood was black and putrid like old rot. Hollow magic exploded in the air — red and black smog twisted around the three of them. Red vines twisted in the gaping hole in the Hollow's stomach, sewing the flesh together.

Shiloh turned his flame towards the Hollow. The golden light surrounded him and burned through the dark smoke shroud. The Hollow shrieked and fell to her knees as the flames took hold, but she still fought it. She clenched her jaw and her fangs dug into the flesh of her lips, but she pushed herself upwards. The Hollow fixed her red eyes on Shiloh.

She pushed forwards, struggling against the pain and flame towards him.

"It's not working," Shiloh said. His eyes were wide with panic. "It's not working!" he said again, tossing a frantic glance to Alix.

"Plan B!" she called out. She threw herself at the Hollow, tackling her to the ground. She wrestled with the weakened beast, rolling around in the bloody sand.

"I have to be the one in the circle!" Shiloh ran around the wrestling pair, making charred marks in the sand with magic. In some places, the sand melted into glass with his touch.

"No. I will do this," Alix growled, punching the Hollow in the jaw.

He said, "This spell wasn't meant for Silvid blood." His words shoved together and breathless with fear.

Shiloh advanced, intending to grab the Hollow off of Alix and push her out of the way, but Alix saw his plans. She slammed the Hollow to the ground and kicked Shiloh out of the way. "Do the spell. I know what I'm asking you to do. Please," she begged, clutching the Hollow.

"Hurry!" Anastasia yelled. "If you can do it, do it! She can't hold her forever."

Shiloh inhaled sharply and stumbled away, nodding at their instruction. Despite his trembling, he chanted words in the ancient tongue. With each word, he spat molten gold. It fell from his lips like lava and pooled at his feet. The air filled with smoke and sparks, and the smell of fire.

Shiloh stepped forward and stretched his arms up to the sky. The space between his hands fizzed and crackled with magic, popping like tiny strikes of lightning. The Hollow caught in Alix's grip suddenly began thrashing, desperately trying to escape, but Alix held on firmly.

The magic at Shiloh's feet crawled to the edge of the circle that Shiloh had drawn around Alix and the Hollow. Once it touched that edge, flames shot up and spread around them, encasing the pair in walls of golden flame. Alix stared at Shiloh, waiting for his signal.

He hesitated, tripped over a phrase, and the flames flickered, but nodded to Alix. She shoved her wrist up against the Hollow's fangs, breaking the skin and letting her blood flow. The golden flames leaped and sank into the blood that slid down her arm.

"Wait!" Anastasia looked between Shiloh and Alix. "No! What are you doing?!" Anastasia lunged forward, trying to break through the flames, but the force of the wind created by the churning flames, like a wall of heat and air, tossed her backwards.

Tears welled in Shiloh's eyes, but the heat of his magic turned them to vapor within seconds.

"Keep going!" Alix yelled, closing her eyes as the magic pulled blood from her wound. She kept her grip on the

Hollow and her blood, glowing with golden light, slowly stretched around the Hollow. It wrapped around her body and tightened like wire, piercing her flesh.

In the center of that circle, Alix stared into the Hollow's eyes and the Hollow stared back. Her lips moved and a single sparkling tear dripped down her cheek.

The golden wire sank deeper into the Hollow's flesh and she shrieked in pain. Alix's blood disappeared into the Hollow and then she was still and silent. The Hollow's eyes locked onto Alix. She smiled and laughed hideously. The sound was more of a bark, constricted by the Hollow's pain.

Alix looked at the Hollow, and their eyes caught again. The look was only a moment, but it stretched on, until finally the Hollow relaxed with a ragged exhale and lay limp in Alix's arms. She took a shaking breath, clearly exhausted from the fight and blood loss.

Alix collapsed into the limp Hollow. The golden wall of flames flickered and died away, shrinking back into the ground, revealing a perfect circle of murky glass. Anastasia rushed to Alix's side and pulled her away from the Hollow.

Alix waved her hand at Anastasia and pointed to where Shiloh stood. Smoke still plumed from him and he shook as he sank to his knees. Anastasia's eyes went wide, and she ran to him. He stared up at her as she delicately put her hands against his cheeks and checked him for signs of burning.

He was nearly untouched, despite the intense display of magic. "I'm so sorry." He looked towards Alix and caught himself on a sob. "I'm so sorry," he repeated.

"It's okay." Anastasia ran her fingers through his hair, attempting to soothe him.

"You don't understand," he said.

Alix pushed herself up. "But I do." Alix coughed and wiped the grime from her face. "It's okay," Alix said. She looked down at the Hollow, who still lay immobile at her feet. "We need to get her home."

"I'll carry her," Anastasia said.

"No." Alix said roughly, with a wild look in her eyes.

Anastasia stepped back, reaching for her sword, but it wasn't at her side. "Alix?"

"I messed up," Shiloh whispered.

Alix closed her eyes. "No. You didn't." She took a slow, deep breath. The air still smelled of smoke. "You were right. This wasn't meant for Silvids, but what is done is done. It had to be done, and I needed to be the one bound with her." She opened her eyes and immediately dropped them down to the beast at her feet.

Alix groaned at the effort, but she pulled the Hollow up into her arms. Without the smoke that usually covered the Hollows, Anastasia could see her clearly. She was more fae than she would have imagined. She even wore clothes, dark ragged clothes that barely covered her body.

When the wind caught the Hollow's black hair, finally letting the moonlight illuminate her face. Meredith. Alix's fated mate who once rejected her, abandoned her for the Hollow pack. The spell Shiloh performed was a pact, meant for human deals with Fae. The promise he'd bound within the sigils was one of peace — the binder and the bound could not harm each other. If a human had bound the fae and broken the promise, the pact would dissolve, but between two fae, the pact was more permanent. Their fates were now tied. If Alix lived up to her promise to kill Meredith, she would die as well. Neither could live without the other.

"Let's go," Alix said, once again stomping off without giving Anastasia another word.

CHAPTER 8

Lana

Lana opened her eyes, squinting at the warm, flickering light of the room. Her body ached and was stiff from inactivity. Anastasia's memories crowded in her head, blurred and fuzzy, but her whole life spread out in front of Lana in broken pieces.

She sat up slowly, wondering how she'd gotten onto the couch. The room was silent, and she was completely alone. Even Shiloh was no longer unconscious on the bed. *Was he alive?* Hope and dread clashed in her chest.

"Hello," she croaked, her voice hoarse. She swayed to the kitchen and got herself a glass of water, chugging it in only a few moments. She suddenly remembered the hidden door she'd seen Luze slide through. That felt like years ago. She didn't feel herself anymore. She had been in Anastasia's memories too long—her dreams a rush of places and people. And now she had no idea what to do or what to think. Her mother was Anastasia's mother and their mother had taken some part of Anastasia with her. The wall had no hope of working, their mother had said.

"Is that what you want me to do? Is that why you showed me all of that? You want me to save the Silvids? But what about Mom? Do you know where she is? What about Feyville and the Hollows? And Liam might still be unconscious. What about saving you? You're the one supposed to help me..." There was no answer to her questions, and Lana lifted the hands that weren't hers and carefully regarded them.

"Anastasia?" Lana's voice was barely above a whisper. "Are you still there?"

She didn't hear her voice float to the surface, but felt a warm rush of energy from deep within her chest. Anastasia was still present and accounted for, but she was done talking for the day. Lana sighed and stretched her muscles before heading toward the secret door, trying once again to find whatever secret mechanism would allow her passage.

She flinched when the door slid open at her touch. Beyond the door was a long hallway, lined with dim torches. She stepped inside and the door closed behind her. There were only three doors in the hallway—one on either side and one at the very end.

Lana paused and strained her ears to listen, but everything was silent. She tiptoed down the hall and carefully tried the doorknob on the left. Finding the door locked, she moved to the other door.

This door opened easily. She took a deep breath to steady herself. The room reminded her of Creon's council room—one of the many blurry and inconsequential memories that now lived in her head without belonging to her. There was a long table in the center of the room, littered with maps and books and notes. Lana approached the table and looked down at the maps. She recognized one of them as the same map Shiloh had shown Alix and Anastasia before the capture of the Hollow—the event that led to Haven being attacked by the creatures and to Anastasia being put in that spell.

Lana crossed her arms across her chest, rubbing her hands up and down her biceps to warm herself. All of Silvis laid out on the table in front of her. She leaned further down, peering at a map that barely peeked out from under the stack. The label read: *Kaelum.*

Lana hesitantly pulled the map from underneath the rest. It was a small map, but encompassed large swaths of land. In the corner, she noticed a large island labeled in tiny writing. That was Silvis. She ran her fingers across the map, stretching them to touch all the land she had never known existed, all the places her nightmares had never taken her.

She hoped that meant that the rest of Kaelum wasn't quite as horrifying as the desert of Silvis.

"What are you doing here?"

At Luze's voice, Lana whirled around in surprise. He leaned against the wall near the door, watching her.

"I was just trying to find everyone," she said.

"They're obviously not here." Luze gestured around the room. "So, why are you still here?"

Lana looked back down at the map. "I know nothing about this place. My mom lived here. Anastasia lived here, but I know nothing. Everything I thought about my life, my family, was a lie. Who am I anymore?" She looked back up at Luze, who remained silent. Was Liam the only thing in her life that hadn't been steeped in secrets? Her heart twisted at the thought of him. "Where is Liam? Where is my body? And what about everybody else?"

Luze twisted his lips from side to side in thought and then beckoned her to follow him. He led her back out to the hallway and to the locked door. He pulled out a key, inserted it in the lock, and twisted. The door opened on a simple bedroom.

Lana sighed, relief and concern mingling in her chest. On the bed, Liam lay unconscious. Her own body curled next to him. The sight of herself and Liam, face-to-face on the bed, made her feel strange—comforted yet uncomfortable in a way that made her ears hot.

"Why is he still asleep?" She stepped into the room to take a closer look. He was breathing deeply, peacefully. Her body was the same—as if they were both taking a nap on a warm summer day.

"Faerie realms are unpredictable. Some humans can navigate the realm, while others are incompatible. Open-mindedness can play a role in that. I suspect your friend here is quite skeptical?"

Lana nodded and returned to the doorway. Skeptical she could agree with. Liam had never been one to believe in fairy tales and magic. He hated ghost stories, though he'd never tried to logic her out of her fear of the dark. She smiled despite herself. Liam was the kindest person she knew.

Luze continued as he exited the room, ushering her out and pulling the door closed. "There's no need to worry. When you both return to the mundane world, he should be just fine. He gestured for her to follow him down to the last door at the end, to what Luze told her was the viewing room.

Shiloh reclined in a heavily cushioned chair and Vas paced nearby. Their attentions were both focused on the city beyond the window.

Lana froze in the doorway as she saw the shadows that leaped into the town square. Hollows were out in droves, jostling and jumping, covering almost every inch of the plaza. They howled and screeched toward the roof of the city hall. She'd never seen so many Hollows; not even in any of her nightmares had they ever been this concentrated or diverse. She had mistakenly thought the wolf-like beasts were the only kind.

Even after seeing the humanoid Hollow at the stable and in Anastasia's memories, she hadn't imagined there would be such a grotesque variety. Some had great, smoke-covered wings. Others stood on two feet, but had short, squashed faces, like pigs or wrinkly dogs. A few Hollows that stood together on an overturned building were almost beautiful in a dark, monstrous way. They were like the captured Hollow in Anastasia's memories—more human-like than the rest.

The humanoid Hollows watched the crowd with veiled amusement. From atop the city hall, a cry sounded. Lana jerked at the familiar sound. Anastasia's memories flooded to the surface again at the sight of the familiar Hollow, standing with a fierce grin at the top of the building. She gave a low, wicked bow, and her short black hair swung forward. Shadows played across her skin, making the bright red of her eyes stand out. Lana squinted as pain jolted through her head at the sight of the Hollow.

Memories twisted painfully, too blurred to understand, so Lana did what she did best — ignored it and pushed it into the dark recesses of her mind.

When the Hollow stood again, she was no longer alone on the roof, but what stood beside her was no Hollow. Or at least Lana didn't think he was a Hollow. There were none of the mysterious wisps of magic that shrouded the Hollows on the man who stood there. He had dark hair and even darker eyes, but his ears pointed like Luze and Vas's.

Luze pushed Lana forward into the room, ushering her to stand beside Shiloh. When she stumbled and hesitated, he whispered, "The Hollows cannot see or hear us."

Lana relaxed somewhat and continued to watch the scene before her. The man on the roof seemed to talk to the Hollow. When he stopped speaking, the Hollow turned toward the crowd and made horrible, gravelly noises that hurt Lana's ears. The noises felt almost like words, almost like speech, but there was a sharp weight to them that felt like she was drowning in knives.

Shiloh leaned forward and placed a finger against his cheek. His focus was on the man on the rooftop. "It's Athan, isn't it? Do you recognize him?" Shiloh asked softly.

"I'm afraid I do," Luze said.

Vas, who had finally stilled, also stared intently at the man. When the Hollow on the roof stopped its screeching, the others cheered.

"What's going on?" Lana asked.

"They're rallying," Vas grumbled, still pacing and fidgeting.

"Like a pep rally or something?" Lana stared out at the boisterous crowd.

Only Shiloh laughed—a short, breathy noise that was over almost as quickly as it began. "Not quite, but I suppose the same idea applies."

"I hadn't realized they could be organized." Luze leaned against the wall with his arms crossed. "Though I suppose it would make sense of all people to organize them, it would be Athan, but I still don't understand. The Hollow woman on the roof with him. She speaks, has her wits. How is that possible? She looks like a Silvid. How are they becoming so fae-like?"

Shiloh sighed. "This really isn't my problem."

Luze cut him a sharp glance. "You promised to help Lana. Her family won't be safe until the Hollows aren't after her anymore."

Shiloh waved his hand. "I'll keep my word, but we couldn't withstand the forces of the wild Hollows. How are we to combat the Hollows now?"

Lana doubled over as a sudden surge of radiant power shot through her body, burning her skin. She closed her eyes against the light that fought to the surface. When she spoke, it wasn't of her own will.

"I will face them again."

Shiloh stood, pushing himself up from the couch with force. His gaze focused on Lana, still crouched on the ground, hiding her face against her knees and clutching her throat.

Luze pushed away from the wall and approached carefully. "What do you mean?"

"We find my mother, restore me, and I will face them."

"Anastasia?" Shiloh asked tentatively.

Lana looked up. Her eyes blazed with golden light. She wore a fierce expression that Shiloh must have recognized.

He smiled and stepped forward, but as he neared, the golden light flickered and faded, leaving Lana to relax back onto the ground. In the last moments, she heard Anastasia's voice tickle her mind before fading completely. *Find her. We'll save the Silvids together and get rid of the Hollows for good.*

Shiloh clenched his fist and turned away angrily. His gaze fell back on the rioting Hollows.

Vas stared at her with wide eyes. "What was that?"

Luze stifled a smile.

"She wants to find Mom and help the Silvids fight the Hollows," Lana said.

Shiloh scoffed. "Fight the Hollows? I'm sure she does. She never wants anything good for her."

"Is no one going to explain anything to me?" Vas asked.

Shiloh chuckled coldly. "It's more than you need to know."

Vas glared at him.

Shiloh merely grinned back. They stood face-to-face, a showdown of sorts. Shiloh lifted a finger and playfully tapped the tip of Vas's horn that ended just below his ear. "You're more beast than man, aren't you?"

Vas stiffened.

Luze held up his hand to silence them both.

Shiloh wore a bitter expression that looked unnatural on the face she'd seen through Anastasia's eyes. Lana frowned, blinking away the remnants of Anastasia's presence.

"What happened to you?" Lana asked, carefully considering his appearance and how different he looked from Anastasia's memories. "You weren't like this before. Anastasia..."

Shiloh's lips tightened into a thin line.

"People change when they lose people they love. Time makes ample ground for shadows to take root," Luze said, though he never took his eyes off Vas.

Shiloh cut his eyes toward Luze and changed the subject. "Do you know where Elaine is, then?"

Lana shook her head. "She disappeared years before I ended up here. We never knew what happened." Lana paused, recalling her own sudden appearance in Kaelum. "Do *you* know where she is? The portal that appeared the night she disappeared looked a lot like the one you made when you brought me here."

"While the spell on Anastasia was in place, any mage could open a portal. Elaine probably opened that one herself." Shiloh shifted toward the windows, staring out at the plaza. "She could be anywhere. What did Anastasia tell you?"

"Anastasia *showed* me how you betrayed her. How you both betrayed her by weakening the spell to supposedly save her. You knew the wall would never hold if our mother put Anastasia in the amulet."

"That's not entirely true. The draining matrix should have easily sustained the spell without her soul. It also helps that Elaine stole Creon's magic."

"Did he know what you two did?" Her sacrifice had been her own decision. She clutched at her chest. Stealing magic meant taking part of someone's soul. In doing that, her mother had sentenced Creon to an early, and painful, death—a withering away.

"Does it matter?" Shiloh asked.

Lana paused. Her thoughts shifted to her childhood. Creon had been her father too before he died, and then her mother had married Marty. He had been loving, but still distant. All her life, her father had been sickly and now she knew why. But her own memories mixed with Anastasia's, who hadn't known Creon as anything but a stern taskmaster—training her to be a warrior with no concerns for her own desires and feelings.

Creon had been the one to suggest the spell in the first place, to suggest Anastasia be the martyr that let the Havenites escape. Lana felt overwhelmed with fragments of Anastasia's memories, but in all of them, her feelings about Creon, who was the leader of Haven before he was ever a father or husband, were complicated. She saw him as a leader, not a caring father.

Another memory flashed across the surface of Lana's mind. Creon's last words to Anastasia — *"I'd readily give my very soul to spare my daughter from pain."* In the end, had Elaine really stolen his magic, his soul, or had he willingly given it to his martyr daughter? She fought back the sting of tears as they welled at the edges of her vision.

"Your silence answers for you." Shiloh shrugged. "Your mother never liked him much, anyway. I doubt she kept him around for long after entering our ancestral lands. Really, without his magic, I don't think he could have possibly survived as long as she has. Magic does that, though. Drains, takes, gives, revives, kills, creates, lives." He turned back to her. "Does that matter, either? Do you care if she betrayed him? After all, he's gone. But what will you do about your mother?"

Instead of answering any of those difficult questions, Lana simply said, "I had a dream she was in a library underground. Here in Haven."

Shiloh shook his head. "All the Haven libraries have collapsed since the exodus decades ago. Perhaps it was just a memory."

Lana chewed on the corner of her lip. It hadn't seemed like a memory, and it had been before she and Anastasia had been joined, but she didn't have any other explanation. Maybe it had just been a dream. So, she nodded.

"May I interject?" Luze interrupted, finally tearing his eyes away from the confused statue that was Vas.

Shiloh watched Luze, daring him to speak carefully just with the set of his gaze.

Luze merely smiled at him. "Where would Elaine go if she returned here? Which it seems likely that she did."

"The garden," Lana said, softly. Her mother had always loved the garden at home. If she'd lived in Haven, she must have had one here.

Luze's face lost the edge of his smile as he looked at Lana. She must have surprised him.

"Then that's where we shall go. But first we decide how to get there."

CHAPTER 9

Lana

They all sat in the room of windows, discussing the layout of the city and the exact location of Elaine's garden. Lana wasn't surprised to discover that her mother's idea of home in Kaelum wasn't the place she had lived with Creon. Her home was a garden on the far side of the city. Among the people of Haven, she was well-loved and known as Lady Haven of the Garden.

Shiloh didn't question Lana again about what had happened with her and Anastasia. Instead, Lana was mostly left out of the conversation. She wasn't alone in that. Vas sat in the corner with a deep frown. His arms were crossed, and he kept his gaze on the city beyond the room, which had finally emptied of Hollows.

Lana sat down beside him while Shiloh and Luze figured out how to get to the garden, especially now that they knew the Hollows were in the city in droves.

"I thought this place was safe." Lana's voice was low, meant only for Vas.

Vas glanced at her. "Yeah. Apparently not. I think he knew it already. Though, don't you think it's odd? Why didn't he want me to come down here with you? And then why not tell me what had happened to Anastasia? Why didn't you tell me? You're in her body with her soul."

"I didn't, and don't, trust you," Shiloh said. "That is why I didn't want you to come with us. Luze is already one too many fae in my home." He stopped and sighed, shaking his head before continuing to talk to Luze, pointing at a map of the city they had on the back wall.

"It was complicated. My soul is trapped in her body, but only a piece of her soul is here. I don't really understand it myself. I'm sorry. I really am her sister though. We have the same parents, even if I never met her." She lowered her voice, hoping Shiloh wouldn't hear. "But I still don't understand why he didn't want you to come with us." Lana, sitting on the floor, pulled her knees to her chest and rested her cheek on her knee. "Is the war so bad to be this paranoid?"

Vas shrugged. "Magic has a way of making people paranoid."

"Especially Brynian magic," Luze added, briefly turning away from Shiloh to look down at her.

"Because you can turn into a horse?" Lana asked. It seemed ridiculous. Who would be paranoid about a horse?

Luze laughed. "Yes, and then some. We are people of dreams. Our illusions obscure. We become. We are everything Silvids wish to tame. Their magic is like this," Luze pointed out to the city. "Stone cities and manipulating the earth and the wilderness. But Brynians? We are the wild, the unknown fantasies and illusions of dreams."

Shiloh rolled his eyes and folded up the map, shoving it in a bag that had been lying across the back of the chair he sat in earlier. "What he really means to say is the Brynians are unpredictable shapeshifters with a talent for illusion, among other things."

"I am not unpredictable!" Vas lifted his lip in a snarl.

Lana furrowed her brows. He seemed on edge, ever since they'd arrived at Shiloh's apartment under the fountain.

"Though you are obviously a beast," Shiloh said.

Vas snapped his jaws shut and turned away. His biceps flexed as he tightened his arms across his chest.

"We best be on our way," Luze said, cutting a reproving glance at Shiloh.

"How are we going to get there?" Lana asked.

"Simple," Shiloh said. "We're going to go straight through the heart of the city and then take the vents up to the garden. I rarely go to Elaine's upper garden. The vents are quite unpleasant." Shiloh rifled through his bag, frowning as he threw it onto his back and started for the door back to his home.

"And what if she's not there?" Lana didn't dare hope it would be so simple, that her mother would be so close.

"Then we look somewhere else. We look until we find the amulet, until I can bring Anastasia home." He muttered to himself about workshops he hadn't searched in years and other places that Elaine might hide an amulet.

"Isn't there some kind of magic, like the mirrors, to find her?" Lana asked.

Shiloh didn't answer. He continued through the door, back to the rest of the house.

Luze was the one to respond. "Your mother doesn't want to be found, it seems. Any magic we've tried has come up empty."

It made sense that her mother would be cautious. What if the wrong person found her? "What about the Hollows?" Lana asked.

"So full of questions." Luze smiled. "I'm sure you'll figure something out."

"Are you not coming?" Lana furrowed her brows. It would be quicker to take Luze's enormous horse-form across the city, wouldn't it?

"Oh, no. Of course not. I've been a pack mule once this week. I don't intend to do it again. Besides, I have my own tasks. I'll double check the libraries, just in case, since you had that dream."

Lana frowned. "But..."

Luze shook his head and gestured toward the door. "You both should get bags together."

Lana sighed and walked through the door, with Vas close behind her.

"You know, you could probably just leave if you wanted to," Lana said. "You don't have to put up with their antagonizing."

"And go where?" Vas said. His face was distant and sad.

"Where were you before? How did you get to the temple? The spell wall was functioning until just before you arrived."

They were alone in the hallway. Luze had stayed in the room of windows and everything was silent.

"I walked."

"Obviously, but why were you in the desert?"

Vas looked away and rustled a hand through his hair. "Being stupid, I guess. I just wanted to prove myself and ended up being more of a failure than I was before." His shoulders were tight, drawn almost up to his ears.

Lana frowned and patted his arm. She left her hand on the warm skin of his arm for a moment longer before she let it drop away. "I won't interrogate you. I don't think you're a bad guy like Shi does."

Vas's cheeks darkened in an awkward blush before he pushed forward down the hallway. "Thank you," he whispered.

Lana smiled and followed him. She wasn't sure what to make of her flock of magical beings. All she knew was that her mother was probably somewhere in this city, filled with Hollows that would love to tear into her. Lana grimaced, hoping the Hollows hadn't already found her mother.

When they entered the main room again, Shiloh already had three bags packed.

"How far away is this place?" Vas stood off to the side.

"Far enough," Shiloh responded, snapping the bags shut. "And the city won't exactly be easy to navigate."

"Great." Vas spoke gruffly, but moved forward and took a bag when Shiloh pushed one in his direction.

With bags hastily packed, Shiloh moved to a tall bookshelf in a far corner. With ease, he pushed the bookcase aside. It seemed to roll on wheels, gliding silently. The bookcase revealed a set of stairs that led up toward the surface. Somehow, Lana wasn't surprised to find that Shiloh had another hidden passageway in his home.

Shiloh started up the stairs, not waiting for them to follow, but they did. Soon they were in a winding hallway. After a distance that Lana was sure spanned most of the city's plaza, the hallway sloped upward and became a short flight of stairs that ended in a single door. Shiloh stopped at the door and motioned them to be silent and still. In that stillness, he listened with his ear turned toward the door and his eyes closed, leaning against the door.

After a stretch of breathless moments, Shiloh relaxed. He opened his eyes and looked over at Lana for a moment in consideration before stepping aside.

"Open the door," he requested, gesturing for Lana to step forward.

She furrowed her brows, but did as he requested. At her touch, the door handle flared with a faint golden light.

"Interesting," Shiloh murmured.

Gears turned and clicked with an unseen, slow mechanical noise. Then the door creaked open. Beyond the door was another room, a library. Bookshelves lined the walls. Tall shelves reached up to the ceiling, turning the room into a darkly oppressive maze.

Lana had no idea how large the room was or where the room was in the city. Shiloh stepped out first and held a finger to his lips. They followed him in silence. Lana usually enjoyed libraries. They reminded her of Liam. Her heart dropped and twisted at the thought of Liam. He should be sitting in a library like this, reading some dusty book, living a normal life, but instead, he was unconscious in Kaelum, because of her.

Lana sighed, wrapped in her own guilt over Liam.

Shiloh glared at her, holding his finger to his lips again.

She wondered why they needed to be quiet. *Could there be Hollows somewhere in the library?* Her blood ran cold at the thought.

The walkways between the shelves were narrow. Vas turned to the side and carefully shuffled behind them, just to avoid scraping his shoulders against the shelves and causing an avalanche of books.

Lana shivered and wrapped her arms around herself. Prickly hairs rose on the back of her neck, and fear kept her from looking in the corners of the room. She'd felt this before, back home, where the shadows seemed to stare without eyes.

Lana twisted her head slightly, trying to look up at the tops of the shelves without being obvious. Only books and shelves stretched up into the ceiling. Lana let out a slow breath, letting herself relax for a moment.

There was nothing there, but the feeling of being watched didn't cease. With each turn they made, the weight of eyes on her grew heavier. She jerked her head from side to side, trying to find the source of her discomfort, but there was nothing.

Vas placed a hand on her shoulder and gave her a lopsided smile. He leaned forward slightly. His voice was barely audible, just a breath against her ear. "I'll keep you safe. Don't worry."

Her ears heated in that strange way, sending an entire flock of butterflies racing through her veins. She squeezed her eyes shut. He was too close. She could still feel the heat of his body just behind her. When she opened her eyes again, she reminded herself that whatever she felt it wasn't hers. Vas belonged with Anastasia. She exhaled roughly and tried her best to ignore his presence.

Shiloh glanced backward at them with a sharp look, though he couldn't have heard more than the rush of her breath. Up ahead, a door finally appeared in the vast expanse of bookshelves and Shiloh made a straight line for the door.

A fluttering sound, like the rustling of pages, came from the top of a nearby bookshelf, and Lana's heart jumped into her throat.

Shiloh paused again at the door, as he had before they entered the library, listening. He didn't close his eyes this time, but he waited much longer than Lana would have liked before he turned the handle. The fluttering sound returned and grew louder as a large black shape plummeted down toward them.

Lana jerked toward the floor as a black bird swooped over them and soared into the empty street beyond the door. The bird disappeared up into the darkness above the city. Lana almost laughed at herself. She'd been terrified of a crow.

Shiloh stepped out into the street, ignoring the crow and its disappearance, seeming unbothered by it, perhaps even familiar with the bird.

Lana and Vas followed, staring into every dark corner of the alley they were in. Vas often glanced upward, searching the rooftops for the dark silhouette of the bird, but it was gone, leaving Lana with uneasiness in the pit of her stomach.

She dared a glance back toward the library and noticed a sign that dangled above the door that had the same sort of lettering from the entrance to Haven and a small stack of books. Anastasia's memories and mind still blended slightly with Lana's, meaning she could read the sign, though it took her longer than she expected. They had just emerged from a bookstore—Golden Books, a surprisingly intact store, considering the state of the street they were now in.

Rubble littered the road and sidewalks. Moss and vines grew up around the stone, reclaiming the city for nature. Shiloh stood still, waiting with alert eyes on the cracked sidewalk. This alley was darker, somehow, than even the rest of the city, despite the blue glow of the moss that covered much of the nearby wall.

The shadows stretched far across the street. After another moment's breath, Shiloh motioned for them to follow as he plunged into the shadow, almost disappearing from sight. Vas and Lana followed, moving quickly to stay near Shiloh, who moved almost too fast for them to stay close and still silent.

They kept moving, and Vas occasionally threw an upward glance at the skyline. Lana followed his gaze and the weight of something pressed down on her, a foggy tingle that left goose bumps on her flesh. It almost reminded her of the feeling of Anastasia's flames or being near Luze when he shifted. But this wasn't warm and light, like Shiloh's magic, or the magic Anastasia could do. This magic tasted different.

At first, it was playful and light. She was caught in it, still staring upward, barely keeping herself from running into Shiloh's back as he continued to lead them through the narrow, dark alleyways of the city, which he seemed incredibly familiar with. As Lana let the strange magic wash over her, there was an aftertaste of rot.

She shuddered and pulled her gaze from the skyline, but the tainted touch of the magic didn't leave her. She pressed her tongue against the back of her teeth, rolling it across the edge as if to scrape away the taste of it. Blood and death.

A sudden laugh echoed from the roofs, bouncing from building to building. Shiloh froze at first and then quickly turned and yanked Lana into the ruined awning of a nearby building to take shelter from prying eyes. Vas ducked down behind them, hiding underneath what was left of the stone archway.

"You cannot hide from me," said a male voice in a playful tone. He laughed again, and the sound drifted down from a broken stone pillar nearby.

Lana held her breath and peered around the edge of their hiding place.

The man—the same that stood by the Hollow on the rooftop—slid down to the ground with a thud. He was heading straight toward them. Dim light cast shadows across his face. He smiled. A grin stretched across his face, revealing fangs that looked unnatural in his mostly human-looking face.

"Fee-fi-fo-fum, I smell the blood of a—" Athan took a deep breath, holding his nose up to the wind. He stopped walking and closed his eyes. The vicious smile grew wider, stretching across his face. He was a marvel of insanity. "You actually woke the girl? Perhaps the traitor was some help to you at last then. I saw you brought some humans over. But to think it was successful in more ways than one..."

Shiloh paled and pressed himself tighter against the stone.

"I'd always hoped you would," Athan said. "The wall was an annoyance." He laughed. "It has stopped nothing, as I'm sure you know, but it was such a nuisance."

Vas crept carefully around behind, switching his vantage point. He picked up a large piece of rubble and hefted it to his shoulder like a shotput.

"I'm sure now the Hollows will gather at the edge of the desert to push forward back into Silvis. Such a shame, really. All that slaughter? If only we could have lived in harmony." Athan sighed dramatically.

They all remained silent and hidden, with Vas ready with his rock.

Athan crossed his arms and stared into the dark with an annoyed exhale. "Just come out. If I meant to hurt you, I would have by now. You're not as stealthy as you'd like to think."

They didn't move.

Athan roared, a sound that made Lana cower. It was unnatural coming from a human throat, but he wasn't human. His eyes flashed red, and fog whirled at his feet. The same dark smoke that covered the Hollows. "Come out," he said. "Before I come get you."

"Run," Vas said as he stood and hurled the rock at the man's head.

Hearing Vas speak, the man turned toward his voice, only to be met with the rock soaring through the air. The rock connected, taking Athan by surprise. It knocked him off-balance, but he didn't fall over.

Shiloh bolted up and grabbed Lana's wrist, dragging her behind him. Vas brought up the rear, running behind them. Lana pulled her wrist free from Shiloh with a jerk. Daring a glance over her shoulder, Lana saw Athan change.

His eyes flared red, and a red light washed over him. Smoke twisted up from his feet, obscuring him, but only for a moment before a red-eyed Hollow beast panther leapt out with a howl. The Hollow panther was much larger than any natural panther should be, and red vines twisted around its body and the length of its tail.

Lana screamed as he bounded after them with a hungry frenzy. Shiloh pulled them through tight turns and crumbling buildings, in an effort to at least put some obstacles in Athan's way.

She had no intention of becoming cat food tonight.

"There's no way we can outrun him!" Vas shouted above the screams of the chasing panther.

"Obviously!" Shiloh ducked through a narrow opening into a nearby building.

Lana scrambled after him quickly.

Vas hesitated at the opening. "Get her out of here. I'll deal with him."

Shiloh glanced at Vas and scoffed. "Idiot." He continued into the building, dodging rubble and ruined furniture.

Lana wavered, staring at Vas with a frown.

"Go," he said with a soft smile. "I'll find you soon. Remember, I said I'd keep you safe."

The panther's screech was nearer now, almost on top of them. Lana turned toward Shiloh, who had now stopped at the opposite side of the room, gesturing for her to hurry.

"Come on. I'm sure he can handle himself. Let's go."

Despite the urge deep in her soul to stay at his side, Lana backed away.

A wave of purple, ghostly light rushed across Vas's body before she turned away and ran. Remembering Vas's failed attempt to shift in the temple, she only hoped this would go better and she was making the right decision, when all she really wanted to do was throw herself between him and danger again.

CHAPTER 10

Vas

Even as the shift took hold, Vas couldn't keep his eyes off of Athan. Something was wrong with him. Despite looking so much like he had, there was the spark of insanity in his eyes and the way his lips curled into a smile too big for his face.

The magic flowed into Vas, but it felt wrong. Shifting had once been like breathing, but now something felt shattered inside him, like a piece of himself was missing. His hands shifted into claws; fangs elongated in his mouth. He was stuck mid-transformation when Athan, as a panther wrapped in shadows and red sparks of Hollow magic, barreled into him, full force, knocking the wind out of him. Athan's claws scraped across his chest, tearing his shirt and drawing blood.

Vas latched onto Athan, wrapping his arms tightly around the panther and digging his claws into the flesh of Athan's back. The panther screamed, and the sound rang painfully in Vas's ears. He wished now that he'd learned more battle magic instead of illusions. When he went into the desert so long ago, he'd relied on his shifting too much.

Vas fought against Athan's weight. *If only he could shift into something big.* He imagined his body expanding, exploding beneath the panther until he was free. With all his willpower, Vas focused on that image, forcing it into existence. Athan yowled as his body was thrown, somersaulting through the air as Vas suddenly shifted. Vas's body grew until he was a giant looming over Athan.

He'd accomplished something he'd never done before — a lesser form of fae-shape shifting. From stolen books and Athan's lessons, Vas had learned that changing sizes was a type of fae-shape shifting. Though it wasn't something relegated to myth, it was still a rare talent. Hope sparked to life in Vas's chest. Did this mean he could finally shift away his horns? Was fae-shape shifting possible for him?

Athan righted himself quickly, but hesitated as he stared at Vas. In an instant, Athan's shift dropped away, leaving him standing with a vicious grin full of pride.

"*Behydan*," Vas said in a struggled breath. He felt the illusion take hold, but as his body faded from view, he lost control of his shift; with an agonizing pop, he reduced to his normal size. Shifting had never hurt before. *What had happened to him?* He was concealed, but no longer a giant.

"Don't run, my prince," Athan said.

Vas barely recognized him. His father's advisor had been the picture of perfection in every way, but this Athan? He wore his hair down, long and untamed, a wildness that matched the look in his eyes.

"What happened to you? How can you shift? You're a Silvid," Vas whispered.

Athan jerked his head toward the sound of his voice. His eyes bored into Vas, making his heart thunder in his chest with fear that the concealment spell had failed.

"A great many things happened," he said. "I don't want to fight you, Vasileios. Come with me, and I'll tell you everything you've missed over the last twenty-five years."

Twenty-five years. The words bounced around his head, echoing in the dark recesses. For a moment, he hesitated. Athan had been his mentor, his beloved teacher, and close friend to his father. But he'd seen him with the Hollows in the square, and there was a strange madness clinging to him. He didn't see the Athan he once knew in the eyes of the man standing before him. "Come with you? You're working with the Hollows!"

Athan raised his hands in a placating offering. "They aren't the beasts you think they are. King Dae made the Hollows this way, but they can be more than hungry animals. Let me show you." He stood in the middle of a clearing between two buildings. Rubble surrounded them on all sides.

"What about my father? Is he really working with you?" Vas kept up the concealment spell and moved in a circle around Athan, trying to move as quietly as possible to avoid detection.

Athan stepped forward, somehow moving closer to Vas, even as he changed directions.

Could he see him, somehow?

With each word, Athan took a step, as if approaching a feral cat. "Would you come with me if he was? If even your father saw the Hollows were just as fae as you and me?"

"Tell me, please," Vas said. "Is he alive, at least?"

"He's alive," Athan said, as he threw his hands up in the air.

Vas could feel the magic in his movement. *What was he doing?* Vas scrambled away, fear seizing him.

The ground shot up around Vas, trapping him in a prison of stone bars. He stumbled back, panicked at the sudden magic, and his back slammed into the stone. Vas couldn't believe his own eyes—Silvid magic.

"Don't you remember? Just like when you were a little bird, I can still see you." Athan laughed, clenching his outstretched hand into a fist. The stone walls tightened until Vas couldn't move. "I can teach you to see as I do, if only you'll let me. I can see the magic pulsing in the air, my prince."

Vas let the concealment spell fade and bared his teeth. He pushed at the stone with all his strength, begged his magic to do something, anything to free him, but nothing happened.

His magic was a tornado inside his chest that wouldn't obey. Anastasia's face kept appearing in his mind, but it was Lana's laughter he heard with her smile. He didn't know which one was his mate, but he'd finally found her. He wouldn't let Athan take that from him.

"Tsk tsk." Athan waggled a finger in the air as if Vas were just a naughty child. "I don't want to hurt you, Vasileios, but I can. I have more magical knowledge, more power—" His eyes lit up. "Let me show you, make you understand why you'd be better off with me!"

Athan held his arms out to the side, throwing his head back in cruel laughter, as water appeared from the air and swirled around his arms. A strong wind howled through the rubble, swallowing Athan's laughter. Purple smoke rose from the stone at Athan's feet.

Athan dropped his gaze to meet Vas's as he shouted into the wind, "*Geefenlaecan*." In a purple glow, Athan duplicated—one man becoming an illusion of three. "Do you understand now?" all three said in unison.

Vas stared unblinkingly as his heart raced. "You're Silvid," he said. "Silvid," Vas repeated. But clearly, the magic in front of him was more than that. *The power of the elements and illusions in one mage? Both Silvid and Brynian? That was possible?* He had once dreamed of having magic from both his mother and father, but he'd been too afraid—he hadn't even understood how Silvid magic worked and no one could teach him. No one had dared to use Silvid magic in the centuries since King Dae sealed the Hollows away.

With a wave of his hand, the wind, the water, the illusions all disappeared and Athan stepped in front of Vas's stone prison. "No, my prince. I am like you, and more." His words hung in the silence.

The realization came slowly. "Half-Brynian. Half-Silvid." Vas stared into Athan's deep-brown eyes and saw for a moment the man who had been his teacher, his confidant, his father's closest advisor.

"And Hollow," Athan added.

"That's not possible," Vas said. "Hollows are beasts. A fae can't *become* a Hollow." *Could they?* He didn't actually know where Hollows came from. *How were they born?* He'd never cared to read the histories or the old legends. He regretted that now.

Athan reached a hand towards Vas, heartache clear in the lines of his face. "It's possible. It's true. I planned to teach you myself, but then..." Athan's sentence went unfinished as a shrieking crow descended from the sky, flying into his face with a fury.

Unable to do anything, Vas watched from his stone prison as the bird flew again and again into Athan's face. Athan yanked his hand up toward the bird, and water engulfed the creature before he threw it to the ground.

Upon impact, the bird faded, like mist on the wind, until a soaking fae lay coughing on the ground.

Luze. Vas inhaled sharply and strained against the stone.

"Oh, wonderful," Athan said with a snarl. "Come to play, little brother?"

"Leave the prince alone," Luze said, still struggling to catch his breath.

"No, I don't think so. In fact, I have something much better in mind."

"No," Luze whispered. Defeat was already in the lines of his face. He pushed himself to stand, but before he could even get to his feet, Luze was caught in another stone prison. They were both at Athan's mercy.

"Don't be so grumpy, Lulu. I would never hurt my student," Athan said as he approached Vas with a sigh. "I have so much to teach you, Vasileios. We were meant for greatness. You were meant to rule just as you are — both Nightmare and Dream." Before Vas could respond, Athan waved a hand over his eyes and whispered, *"Beslaepan."*

Vas only had a second to register the spell before he lost consciousness.

CHAPTER 11

Luze

"It's actually quite convenient that you've stopped by, brother," Athan said.

Luze bared his teeth. *When had he started seeing his brother as his enemy, instead of his savior?* He wrapped his fingers around the stone bars of his cage. If only he wasn't so weak... He had the knowledge of tomes' worth of magic, but his ability to act as a conduit for spells was pathetic. Even drawing magic from the environment was challenging for him. It was too soon for him to shift again. His body couldn't handle that sort of space-distorting illusion back-to-back. There was nothing he could do but wait for Athan to decide his fate.

"Quiet as usual?" Athan shrugged. He strolled around the rubble, stopping for a moment to retrieve Vas's unconscious body from the stone prison he'd placed him in. He held Vas in his arms and approached Luze again. "I have a surprise for you, Lulu."

He hated that nickname. He hadn't always disliked it, but ever since things went horribly wrong in the Silvid Court, Athan had only used that name to mock him.

"A shame you don't want to chat with me. It's been so long since we've seen each other, hasn't it?" Athan shifted Vas in his arms, cradling his head against his shoulder. With a protective hand resting against his forehead, as if Vas were a small child. "Ah well. We'll be seeing much more of each other from now on, little brother."

"What do you mean?" Luze leaned into the stone bars, wishing he had the strength to snap them apart.

"That's what gets a rise out of you?" Athan's brow rose. "You'll see soon, but for now, look at my surprise!" Athan took a step back, muttering a long string of ancient magic beneath his breath. Purple sparks cracked through the air, and Athan changed. His hair smoothed and lengthened. His height shifted, and his face stretched ever so slightly. Even his clothes changed.

In the span of a few moments, Athan was an entirely different person. Luze gasped, eyes going wide as he saw his brother, who now looked exactly like him. It was like gazing into a mirror.

"See you soon, brother," Athan said, as he turned to walk away, wearing Luze's face. "I'm off to satisfy my curiosity and cause a bit of mischief!" He laughed, not bothering to look back at Luze, still trapped in the stone cage, as two enormous wings exploded from his back. Athan leaped into the air with Vas in his arms.

Luze watched as they disappeared into the dark of the cavern.

CHAPTER 12

Lana

Shiloh and Lana stood at the foot of a stone pillar that reached up into the dark recesses of the cavernous ceiling, higher than any skyscraper Lana had ever seen. At their feet, a pit gaped open, plunging into a seemingly endless void. Wind roared from the pit, rushing upward with a howl. Heat radiated from the vent, and Lana took a step back as the stray wisps of wind snatched at her hair and clothes. Shiloh frowned, shifting his gaze up to the hidden height of the pillar.

"We're going up there, somehow, I'm guessing," Lana shouted above the wind and pointed to the top of the pillar.

Shiloh nodded. "Yes, I need to find..." She could barely hear him as the roar of the wind swallowed his trailing words. He turned, taking stock of their surroundings with a frown still firmly set in place. "Ah ha!" He hurried to grab one of two ropes attached to a metal plate. He groaned at the weight of the metal.

Instinctively, Lana reached for the other rope, and together, they pulled it to the edge of the pit.

"Now, we need to tie this off on both sides," Shiloh said as he worked, skirting around the pit.

Lana now noticed the small hooks on opposite sides of the pit.

Taking the rope from her, Shiloh slipped the ropes around the metal hooks, looping them through a center hole, but not yet pulling them tight. "Come, be useful."

Lana hurried to help, and Shiloh shoved one rope in her hand.

"At the same time, we pull," he said. With the weight of the metal and screaming over the wind, Shiloh's face flushed from exertion.

Lana nodded and readied herself for the task.

"Pull!" Shiloh shouted.

They put their weight into the ropes and the metal slid, gliding across the ground until it hovered over the pit, fitting perfectly into the hole. The whole thing reminded Lana of docking a boat, and she got an uneasy feeling about what Shiloh expected them to do.

"Perfect." Shiloh took the rope from her again and wrapped them both around his hand, keeping them taut. He pointed, gesturing for her to stand on the metal.

"What!?" She stared at him blankly as she tried to process the situation. "Why?"

"We're taking the vents up to the garden. You already knew this," he said impatiently.

Wind devoured his words as Lana strained to understand.

"Taking the vents?" Lana stalled for time as she stared at the horrific wind elevator.

"We're riding the winds up, yes. I'd rather not delay long enough for the Hollows to find us." He stepped onto the metal and gestured for her to follow.

Her heart hammered. *A wind elevator that might kill her or Hollows that certainly would?* Lana took a deep breath and decided. She stepped onto the metal, and Shiloh only gave her moments to orient herself before he threw the ropes off to the side and the plate shot upward.

Her feet felt magically glued to the metal, even as they shuddered to a stop at the top of the pillar. Shiloh hopped off and offered his hand to help. Lana didn't waste a moment jumping onto the firm stone beside him. The wind seemed quieter, gentler this high up. She sighed, not daring to think about how they would get down.

"How did we not die?" Lana pressed her fingers against her eyelids, breathing slowly as she fought to calm her terror. Just like with the nightmares, she pushed it down...she ignored it. *It was fine. She was fine.* She exhaled slowly and dropped her hands from her face.

"Magic," said Shiloh blandly. "The metal is enchanted. The ancient Silvids once lived here, so much of their enchantments remain — like this and the water elevator." He grimaced and turned away from her.

The garden stretched before them. It was as if she'd completely left the cavern city of Haven. On the ceiling at the center of the pillar, a hole opened out to the desert far above. Sand trickled down with a gentle hiss and the sun swept away the gloomy blue she'd become accustomed to.

Lana stepped out onto the warm grass, bathed in sunlight. Lush trees swayed in a gentle breeze. Flowers bloomed in a small clearing. Lana wandered forward and let her gaze sweep the garden. In the back corner, a white gazebo nestled against the trees. A wooden bridge with stained glass decorating the rails crossed a gap that circled the gazebo. Looking closely, she could see the gap was actually stairs sinking into the ground and spiraling around the gazebo. *Why hadn't they just taken the stairs?* Ignoring her frustration, she continued looking around her mother's garden.

At the edge of the garden was a thin fence, and beyond the fence was the dark, vast cavern that spanned the space between them and the entire city below. The blue light of the city twinkled in the darkness, feeling far away like swaths of starlight. Within the garden, trees clumped together, leaving small meadows that held disused beds, rimmed with stones or tiny iron fences.

Lana inspected a nearby garden bed. Herbs grew wild from neglect. Up above, the sun shone down, and Lana could see the sky. The coppery tang of death that clung to the desert occasionally drifted down on the breeze. Lana looked more closely and noticed what little sand fell toward them disappeared before it ever touched the ground of the garden—more magic, she assumed. She marveled at the beauty and strangeness of this oasis in the city of stone.

Shiloh stood behind her with crossed arms. "How did you get here so quickly?" His eyes were trained on the shadows among a copse of trees.

Lana strained to see who hid in those shadows.

"Flying by the winds of Fate, I suppose." Luze stepped out of the shadows of the nearby trees. He had a playful grin on his face that somehow seemed out of place.

Lana, ignoring the quiet bickering between Luze and Shiloh, refocused on her surroundings. She'd been surprised to see Luze, but relief flooded her as she saw Vas slumped on the ground near his feet.

Lana stepped quickly to Vas's side. Claw marks scraped across his chest, tearing his shirt, that was now matted with blood and sweat.

Lana fussed over him, stumbling with what to do, but Luze clicked his tongue at her.

"He'll be fine. Superficial wound. Fae heal much quicker than humans. He just needs rest."

Lana had a hard time accepting his words, but kept her hands to herself as she sat by his side, watching his chest rise and fall with each breath.

Vas opened his eyes slowly, and a soft breeze rustled his hair. His eyes widened and he scrambled to sit up. "Where am I? How did I get here?" He jerked around, scanning the surroundings.

"I saved you. Calm down, Vasileios," Luze said, and Vas relaxed back onto the ground.

"Have you already searched?" Shiloh asked Luze.

"For what?" Luze furrowed his brow.

"Elaine." Shiloh's impatience sharpened his glare.

"Of course I have. She's not here, unless she's hiding." Luze shrugged.

"Then let's get on with this." Shiloh looked at Lana expectantly.

"What? No. You can't just give up that quickly! Luze said she could be hiding. She might still be here. We haven't even looked. I haven't even looked." Lana dug her fingers into the warm grass. The trees were dense; maybe she was somewhere. She had to be somewhere.

"Then look. See for yourself that she's not here. Then we can start searching Elaine's workshops and stop wasting time."

"What do you expect to find there?" Luze asked.

The lilt of his voice and the sharpness of his smile seemed odd. He almost seemed like another person. Lana shook off the idea, rationalizing that she'd spent too little time with any of them to know their habits and natures.

Shiloh raised his brows and inspected Luze. His eyes searched each line of his face. "I expect to find Elaine and, if not her, then her tools."

"Her tools?" Lana asked. "I thought we were looking for—"

Shiloh cut her off. "Elaine may not wield the flame, but she had magic. Soul magic. Maybe we won't need Elaine to help."

"I won't give up on finding my mother," she said.

"Yes. Yes. I remember. The sooner we get Ana back, the sooner things go back to normalcy," Shiloh said.

Lana fell silent. *What was she even doing anymore?* She watched them all as her emotions threatened to fly from the cage where she kept them restrained—the locked box in the corners of her mind. Shiloh stared into the distance, tapping his foot. Vas stared up at her, concern clear on his face, but Luze was observing Vas. He rubbed his fingers across his jaw and his lips curved into a frown.

"I know she's here somewhere in Kaelum," Lana said.

Shiloh didn't turn around. His hands tightened together. "How do you know? How can you be so sure?"

"She disappeared from our home without a trace. This is the only place she could have come."

"Is it now? Is it really the only place? Perhaps she just ran away, or perhaps..." He turned with a grimace. "She's already dead, torn apart by the Hollows."

Lana shook her head fiercely. "There's no way. I would know. Anastasia would know."

He narrowed his eyes at her. "You are a foolish, naive girl."

"And you're a snooty ice queen." Lana slapped her hand over her mouth, surprised that she'd let that slip out. Being in Kaelum was affecting her self-control.

Shiloh's eyes widened, and Luze burst into a fit of giggles.

"You've got to admit she nailed you there," Luze said.

"Shut up," Shiloh snarled. He turned away from them both and stared again at the abyss, brooding over the darkness of the city.

Lana protested, but her whines became a scream as a group of winged Hollows dropped into the garden from above. Remnants of the setting sun scorched their bodies, completely burning away the shadowy fog that normally clung to their limbs. The injured Hollows swooped down low over the garden, nearly crashing into the trees before they plummeted off the side toward the city.

Vas quickly grabbed Lana, placing his hand across her mouth to quiet her screams. He shushed her and held her tight.

Lana's heart thundered, and she was suddenly too aware of where his skin touched hers. His warmth radiated through her, like a calming and familiar embrace.

Despite the situation, she wondered whether their closeness also affected him, but his eyes remained fixed on the hole leading to the desert sky above. Frustrated war cries floated from the desert.

A woman's voice rang above the rest, cursing and jeering toward the hole.

"Hurry! Follow the blood trail. It'll lead us to the den," the woman cried.

Shiloh looked at Luze with wide eyes and suddenly rushed forward, urging them all into the underbrush to hide. Vas let go of Lana, but his release was slow, almost as reluctant as Lana felt.

They all crouched in the trees, hiding in brambles as a small troop of soldiers began a rope descent into the garden.

Lana watched intently. The woman's voice had sounded somewhat familiar, but not like her mother's. It had been years, though, and she was realizing now that nothing was as she thought it was. So, she watched, hoping somehow her mother was the woman descending into the garden from the cruel desert.

The soldiers slid carefully down their rope and into the garden. It was a group of four. They all wore similar armor, Silvid armor. Three of the soldiers wore helmets that obscured their faces, and stood in rigid patience, waiting for commands.

The fourth soldier stood at the front, helmetless, with her face on display. Lana recognized her immediately. She was a mountain of a woman, tall and broad. Though she wore Silvid-style armor, her breastplate was emblazoned with the crest of Haven. She was the only one in the group not wearing a helmet, and didn't seem to have one with her at all. Her ashen-blonde hair was braided tightly away from her face, which was scarred and fierce with purpose. She scanned the garden with keen precision. This was the woman from her last nightmare—General Bludeg.

The warm flutter in her chest that she had come to associate with Anastasia kicked into a roaring fire at the sight of Alixandra Bludeg. Without thinking, Lana shoved to her feet. Surprised, Shiloh's attempts to grab Lana and pull her back down were unsuccessful. She stumbled out into the clearing toward Alix.

At the sudden noise of Lana's approach, the soldiers all shifted into formation, pulling weapons out and pointing them toward Lana. Alix stood at the front, brandishing her sword. It was the same sword she had always used, even in sparring matches with Anastasia.

The war-hardened expression on Alix's face faltered as Lana stepped into view.

"Anastasia?" Her voice was soft, unusual for Alix.

Lana came to a sudden stop as she realized Alix didn't know her, and she didn't really know Alix, either. The memories she had of her were Anastasia's.

In the warm sunlight, Alix's eyes met Lana's.

Her demeanor shifted. Alix's face twisted into anger, and she swept her gaze around the clearing. "What have you done? Where are you?" She stormed into the trees, slashing at the tall grasses with her sword, regardless of what might hide there, to become a victim of her careless blade.

"Wait! Wait!" Lana chased after her. "Please."

Alix turned sharply toward her, a reddish tinge in her eyes. "What did he do to you?" Her words came out rough and snarling.

"Nothing you wouldn't have done if you'd known how." Shiloh stepped from the underbrush.

Alix brandished her sword as she stepped toward him, easily closing the gap between them. He just barely stepped out of her way. She was expecting it. With another fierce smile, she twisted around behind him, but kept her sword in front of his body, ending with the sharp blade at his throat and his body trapped against her.

"I never liked you. She never saw the snake you were, underneath all your adoration." Alix's words came out as more of a growl than speech.

Shiloh stood calmly, but completely still. The blade already drew a thin line of blood at his throat. "Such a sweet reunion, friend," he said. "You know you would have done the same. I brought her back. The Lady Haven made this possible."

"She was never my lady."

"Yet you still wear her colors?"

Alix pulled her sword away from his neck and put a boot on his back as she shoved him away.

Shiloh stumbled forward, barely keeping himself upright.

"I don't need to explain myself." She sheathed her sword and turned her gaze back to Lana. She inspected her, walking closer and circling her.

Lana stood still, waiting for Alix's inspection to be over.

She stopped in front of Lana and caught her eyes again. They stared at each other for a long time. Alix frowned.

"I meant to break the spell," Shiloh began. "But instead, Elaine's daughter, Lana, has taken up residence within Anastasia."

Alix turned again toward Shiloh with renewed fury.

He held up his hands in surrender and continued. "Anastasia has surfaced. She still takes up space in that vessel, but her soul is not whole. Once we have Elaine's amulet, I believe I can pull her pieces together again and she will be as she once was."

Lana glanced back at their previous hiding place. Luze and Vas listened quietly from the underbrush, their eyes barely visible in the shadows of the trees.

Alix shook her head and turned her gaze toward her soldiers, who still stood at the ready. She lifted her hand in a quick, commanding gesture, and the company sheathed their weapons and stood at ease.

One man stepped forward. His voice was light and dancing, bouncing off the metal of his helm. "General Bludeg, what of our hunt?"

Alix frowned. "We could track the beasts back to the den, but I'm afraid this interruption may take precedence for now. Unless you wish to hunt without me." Alix glanced out into the darkness of the city. "But I don't advise it, Remi."

Remi nodded. "I'll speak to the others about it." He stepped back toward the other soldiers.

Alix turned back to Lana. "You are going to explain everything to me, starting with who you are and ending with here and now, why you are here in the garden."

Shiloh glared at Lana, daring her to speak, but she ignored him. She explained everything to Alix. She told her about her home in the mundane world, her family, Liam. Lana told Alix about her nightmares of the desert and how she'd been whisked away to Kaelum. She told her everything she could think of without leaving out a single detail. With Anastasia's warm presence still bubbling at the surface, Lana felt safer than she had since entering Kaelum. *Alix would make it right. She always knew how to make it right.*

After her tale was done, the sun was fading, casting shadows in the garden. It was likely close to dusk in the desert, but in the garden, dusk had already turned into a dim twilight.

Alix nodded and thanked her for her story.

They all sat against the trees, reclining in the underbrush. Remi and the other two soldiers had opted some time ago to return to their camp above in the desert sands. Now they all sat in quiet contemplation. Shiloh brooded. Luze was nowhere to be seen. Vas sat in the shadows and stared at Lana, his face unreadable.

"So." Alix took a deep breath. "You broke the spell wall?"

Lana nodded.

Alix stretched and slowly got to her feet. "The wall has been weakening in the last decade." She directed a stern look at Shiloh. "I'm sure you've had nothing to do with that."

Shiloh gave a noncommittal shrug.

"Though the wall never stopped the influx of Hollows." Alix looked down at her hands, flexing them in the dim light, stretching the scars that decorated her knuckles and palms.

"Because it was never strong enough and never could be strong enough to keep the Hollows at bay," Shiloh muttered.

Alix raised her brows and let out a mirthless laugh. "No. It was plenty strong. Every Hollow within its walls was completely and irreversibly trapped on this side—until recently, that is. That's not the problem."

"Then what was the problem?" Lana asked.

"Because I was right." Shiloh clasped his hands together in his intellectual victory. "The Brynian king and his advisor are creating Hollows."

Alix furrowed her brows, squinting up her features into a quizzical expression. "What?"

"That's what you're talking about, isn't it? The influx of Hollows? They are being born in Silvis." Shiloh leaned his head back against the tree where he reclined, nodding to himself with satisfaction.

"Well, no, but yes. I don't think I'm following." Alix looked between Shiloh and Lana.

"Then you tell us. Where are the Hollows coming from?" Shiloh asked, his brow arched.

"Do you even know what the Hollows are?" She scoffed. "I would think you would know with your years of study and devotion to magic and all that nonsense before the fall of Haven and now after, during your pursuit of reviving Anastasia. Did you never come across the lore of Hollows?"

"Perhaps I did somewhere." Shiloh looked away, crossing his arms.

Vas blinked, breaking out of his thoughts. "They're fae," he said, still distant and dreamy.

Lana pursed her lips, looking at him with concern. *Was he hurting?* The wounds looked like they were healing, but he seemed so...out of it. She frowned.

"Yes," Alix said, startling a bit at Vas's voice. This was the first time he'd spoken since Alix arrived. With confusion plain on her face, Alix stared at him for a moment, where he sat concealed by the shadows. She shook her head and continued, "They are fae. I am sure you are acutely familiar with the burn of human magic. You use it and push it and come to the edge of your boundaries, at the very limit of your existence, until your very soul and body burst into flames."

"Yes, I am familiar with the concept," Shiloh said, an embarrassed flush creeping up his cheeks.

Alix hesitated before continuing. "The ancients warned of the Hollows. Legends were told by firelight, but no one believed. We all thought it was just a scary bedtime story, an allegory. It wasn't until the wellspring was uncovered that we rediscovered the truth. Unlike humans, we don't have a limit. There are no deadly boundaries to our magic. We are magic, but..."

Alix frowned, but Lana urged her to continue.

"When magic consumes humans, you die in a burst of flames. When magic consumes Silvids, we become Hollow."

Lana thought back to the crowd of Hollows in the city plaza, the beasts that chased her through the desert. She'd thought they were mindless, ravenous beasts, but they were fae, twisted by their own magic. With each death, a Silvid was killed. Each day a new Hollow could be born from someone she knew. *Was there any hope?*

CHAPTER 13

Athan

While the others were lost in conversation, Athan, disguised as Luze, slipped away. For now he had other things to do, and other things to think about. For the last several decades, Athan had been spying on his brother and the mage using a magic mirror in the temple and another in the plaza. But with them moving around so much, Athan would need to consider a new solution. Perhaps something portable. He tapped his chin as he wandered through Haven, heading back to the den.

He'd learned so much just in that short time in the garden. Elaine was hiding. The Keeper wasn't truly woken, and the mage was looking for Elaine's tools to fix it. Ha. He would find the tools first, and find Elaine first. The Keeper wouldn't interfere in his plans much longer.

He chuckled to himself, and disappeared into the shadows of the city.

CHAPTER 14

Lana

"Well," Shiloh said. "That doesn't affect any of us here, except you."

"And when all the Silvids have become Hollows, what force will you raise against them?" Alix spoke calmly with her hands resting, clasped across her knee. Dusk deepened around them, the shadows lengthening in the garden's peace.

"What does it matter? The Hollows aren't my problem." Shiloh shrugged.

Blood drained from Lana's face as Shiloh's words hit her ears. He'd promised to help her, to save Feyville from the Hollows. "You lied to me," she said.

Shiloh's eyes widened, realizing what he'd said. "Lana—"

"You promised to help me! You promised you'd save me from the Hollows!" Lana shook with anger. "What does it matter?" She scoffed.

"And I will save you. I'll do everything in my power to keep you—to keep Anastasia—safe," Shiloh said. "We can't destroy the Hollows. There's too many. Their power is too great, and that's if you, or Anastasia, were even willing to slaughter an entire race of fae. There's nothing you can do. Nothing you could ever do. But I need Anastasia. She's important to me." He turned away, letting the shadows fall across his face and obscure his eyes.

"You lied to me," Lana said again.

"I said I would help you, and I am. Will you not help Anastasia now?" he asked, crossing his arms.

"I'll help her, but not for you." Lana turned back to Alix, resigned to ignoring Shiloh's existence for as long as possible. "How do we stop the Silvids from becoming Hollows?"

"Or cure those already lost?" Vas added.

Lana couldn't help but notice the distant look in his eyes. She wished she could understand him, help him. They had been traveling together for days now, but she still knew nothing about him. She wanted to know everything. The thought startled her, so she immediately shoved it in the little dark box in the back of her mind, where all the unpleasant things went.

"There is something missing here," Shiloh said slowly, rubbing at his jawline in that pondering way he often did. "If only Silvid can become a Hollow, then why is Athan of Brynia wrapped in Hollow vines and perfumed with the dark fog?"

Alix turned her attention to Shiloh, though she didn't look surprised. "Perhaps not even the Brynians are safe from the corruption of magic."

"He's half-Silvid," Vas said, before adding in a whisper, "like me."

The company grew quiet, and Alix's attention focused in on Vas more carefully, inspecting his face that had been draped in shadows until now. "Vasileios? When I heard your voice...though we only met the one time...but...you died..." she trailed off. "You survived the wellspring?"

Vasileios. Golden light leaped in Lana's chest, frothing with a fragile hopefulness.

"I suppose I did," he said, but did not elaborate.

"What am I missing?" Lana clenched her fists against her temples as Anastasia's golden presence battled for dominance as she looked between Alix and Vas.

"Nothing that matters." Vas's gaze dropped to the dirt and his shoulders slumped forward.

Alix tapped her foot slowly. "Let me see your eyes, Prince," she said to Vas. "Have you been using magic?"

"Prince?" Lana furrowed her brows, but they ignored her question. *What did she mean—prince? Prince of what?* Lana couldn't keep track of what was going on. A sharp stab burst through her head like a wildfire, and she leaned forward, twisting her fingers into her hair. Her heart raced with panic at the sudden flurry of emotions that didn't belong to her — recognition, bliss, relief.

My green-eyed prince. Anastasia's golden consciousness butted up against her own. *It really is him! I didn't dare dream he still lived.* Lana struggled against her, the pain of their thoughts running on top of each other overwhelming her. *Let me out!* Anastasia seethed against Lana's constraints, the golden fire burning away her resolve until she simply broke free.

"*Vasileios,*" Anastasia said.

His head jerked up. "Lana?"

Anastasia wrenched forward, her hands searching towards Vas.

"Anastasia? It's really you! What happened? How can this be?" Shiloh pushed to his feet, stumbling over the underbrush as he rushed to her side, but she ignored him, heading straight to Vas.

Vas furrowed his brows until their eyes met, and his confusion melted away. "Your eyes are gold again," he said, as he twined his fingers with hers and a blush darkened his stony cheeks.

She tightened her grip as she scrambled through the grass to sit on the ground beside him. Finally, they were together again. "I thought you were dead..." Tears burned in her eyes and slid down her face, dripping from her chin in thick, joyful drops. She vividly remembered the day a courier had come from the queen's guard to alert Creon of his death. It had been merely two days after they'd captured the rogue Hollow.

Vas brushed away her tears with gentle fingertips. "Hello again," he said with an awkward smile.

She laughed, choking on a sob. "Since we're both trapped in Haven, we'll have time to talk now."

"Every spare moment," he agreed. "Whatever you want."

"I want everything," she said, gripping his fingers against her face.

"Not to break up the reunion, but now is not exactly the time for happy ever afters. We still have the Hollow problem, and I think you're exactly who we need, Anastasia. Your magic could turn the tide," Alix said. She forced a smile to her face, but her eyes were dim.

"Right," Anastasia said. Embarrassment lit her entire face bright red, and she carefully untangled her fingers from Vas.

Shiloh teetered nearby, visibly anxious. He held his hands out, and a gentle golden glow radiated from his face. "No. No, this can't be right. Your soul is too fractured." Shiloh closed his eyes, and the glow intensified.

"I'm fine." Anastasia jerked away from Shiloh. Lana's anger still bubbled in her chest, which was okay, because Anastasia was angry with him too. "It's fine."

"I need you to go back and rest." He reached for her again. "When we get the amulet, we'll fix you."

"I said I'm fine." Anastasia pushed Shiloh's hands away roughly.

"You don't understand. It's dangerous like this. You're at risk of burning," he said. Wind rushed from the desert above, rustling the trees that surrounded them.

"Maybe you should listen to him," Vas said. "Let Lana back out."

"No," Anastasia said. "I'm myself again. Alix is here. You're alive, and we can do something that actually matters. I can save the Silvids with Alix." She couldn't take her eyes off Vas. *Alive. Alive. Alive.* The word repeated in her mind, echoing through the pain she'd felt at his loss all those years ago. Nothing had mattered anymore after she lost him. Something inside her had shattered, but no more.

"Oh, now you don't care about finding your mother? Is there no one you won't abandon for someone else's quest?" Shiloh muttered.

Anastasia ignored him. He was right; she didn't know where her mother was or whether she was even still alive. But even if Elaine were alive, she might not be for much longer if the Hollows had spread beyond the desert.

"There is no cure. I've seen the madness in Hollow eyes. There is no way to return from it. The only way to rid ourselves of this curse is death for the fallen and self-control for those who remain," Alix said.

"Then what are we going to do?" Anastasia asked, rubbing her hands up and down her biceps to bring warmth to her skin. The falling night brought a chill wind into the garden.

Alix turned away, tension in every line of her body as she spoke. "You and I will cut them off at their source—their queen."

"The Hollows have a queen?"

Shiloh laughed. "That's impossible. Even if they were once fae, they are nothing but beasts."

"We saw the Hollows in the plaza. You know that's not true," Anastasia said.

"I've been tracking them. I've been watching them. Each night, I hunt. They have a queen, and I will kill her. Now, with Anastasia, we can go straight to the den."

"You can't possibly be serious. Going straight into the den? That's suicide, especially for Anastasia in the condition she's in," Shiloh said.

"When will you ever listen to what Anastasia wants for a change?" Alix growled. "She's not your pet to follow your whims."

"Shiloh has human magic—soul magic. He can see things we can't," Vas said. "Maybe we should listen to him, at least in this."

"Stay out of this, Vasileios," Alix said, raising her voice with a sudden sharpness. The sound echoed through the cavern, barely muted by the garden's foliage. Alix shifted her body so that she stood between Anastasia and the others. "I'm going to the den with or without help. My soldiers nicked those Hollows with a bleeding poison. All we have to do is follow the trail." Alix glanced over her shoulder. "Are you going to join me, Anastasia?"

Before Anastasia could answer, an angry screech pierced the stillness of the air. Alix drew her sword instinctually and turned toward the source of the noise. In the vast abyss above the city, red eyes had found them in their garden safety. Winged Hollows converged upon them, diving into the garden and weaving between the trees.

The winged Hollows wore shadows and the red sparks like the rest, but instead of smoky fur, their bodies were feather and bone, dripping with inky fog. They brought the scent of decay on the desert wind as they flapped their enormous wings. Sharp black beaks opened to unleash another barrage of hideous screeches.

The creatures swooped, claws seeking exposed flesh. Alix swung her sword, clipping the underbellies of whichever creatures were brave enough to fly near her. Anastasia yanked her sword from its sheath at her side, and her golden fire rippled along the blade in an instant. But something was wrong. Her lungs burned, and she coughed. Black ash flew past her lips. Shiloh was right. Her face paled. She couldn't use magic without burning.

A nearby Hollow turned its glowing glare toward Vas, locking its eyes to his. It snapped its serrated beak, eager to taste flesh.

Fear flooded Anastasia. She'd lost him once. She couldn't bear to lose him again. When it swooped down to sink its claws into him, she dove between them, ignoring the sword that she clenched lifelessly in her hands.

Anastasia screamed as the claws raked across her face. Blood dripped into her vision. Her heart pounded. *Where did it go?* She wiped the blood that continued to run down her face, desperate to see, to stop the tragedy that was unfolding in front of her.

The Hollow dove for Vas with frenzied determination. He roared in pain and anger as the Hollow latched onto him. He swatted at the creature, to no avail. No matter how he jerked or flailed, nothing worked to free him.

Anastasia reached toward him, flames shooting from her fingertips, but she was too late.

Still clutching Vas's arms, the Hollow leaped into the air. Anastasia jumped after him, but her fingers soared through the empty air. The beast flew away, taking Vas with it.

Vas had been taken, and it was her fault. Anastasia stared in shock as Vas was borne up into the dark abyss over the starless city of twinkling blue.

The other Hollows left continued to terrorize them, but Alix swung with her sword until the creatures fell to her blade or retreated in exhaustion. They turned back and sank into the darkness of the city, leaving them alone in the garden with one less member of their company.

Anastasia dropped to the ground and pressed the unused sword into her side as she stared into the darkness. A hundred "if only's" swarmed in her mind, like irritated bees, bees searching for a monarch they lost. If only she'd not thrown herself in front of the creature...if only she'd not been so afraid, so ready to sacrifice her life for his, maybe he wouldn't be gone.

"I'm going with you," Anastasia said in a far-off voice, still battling the "if only's" that crowded her mind. She closed her eyes and easily felt the jagged edges of her soul, the singed pieces that her magic had already consumed. "But, Shiloh is right. I'm too broken. Take Lana instead. I'll help her, but I can't continue like this and live."

Anastasia exhaled slowly. Lana struggled in the dark corners of her mind, so she gave in. She let Lana rise. When Anastasia opened her eyes, they were brown once more.

"Do you even know how to use that sword?" Alix asked.

"No, but Anastasia does," Lana replied, reaching inside herself to grab that golden place inside her mind that Anastasia occupied. Like a honeyed ghost, Lana felt Anastasia's presence—her memories, her soul—sliding into her skin, warming her muscles. She pulled the sword from its sheath and swirled it in the air, slicing impressively before sheathing it again in a fluid, graceful motion.

Alix considered Lana for a moment, frowned, and then nodded. "All right."

"Not all right." Shiloh stepped forward. He moved with less confidence now that Alix was here. He sounded more like the Shiloh that Anastasia remembered. "We have plans. I can't allow you to take her with you. We nearly have her back. Anastasia is almost home. Please."

"And what are you going to do to stop me? To stop her?" Alix crossed her arms.

"Don't you want her home?"

"Anastasia made her choice a long time ago, and I respected that. You've now brought Elaine's second daughter into Kaelum, and she can make her own choices as well."

Lana grinned at Alix, bolstered by the warmth that flowed up from Anastasia.

Shiloh sneered. "And what of your mother? You wanted to help Anastasia and free her from the curse. What of that?"

"You and Luze can find the amulet. I have no idea how to find Mom, no clues to even lead me to where she could be, but I know where Vas is. I am going to save him." Lana turned to Alix, blood caked and drying on her face from the Hollow's scratch. "I'm going with you."

"Then we'll meet back with my men in the desert to rest and strategize."

Shiloh didn't speak. He stared after them as they left—defeated, silent, and alone.

CHAPTER 15

Shiloh

Alone. Shiloh slumped to the ground in Elaine's garden as he watched Anastasia leave, following Bludeg up a rope and into the freezing desert.

You should have known she would abandon you, the Voice grumbled, clawing its way to the surface from the pits of Shiloh's mind.

"Shut up," Shiloh growled.

Your obsession is a sickness. Purge it from your heart and make room for your own fate, it said.

"I'm not obsessed," he whispered.

I assume you would say it's love, then?

"No—well, yes, but..." Shiloh sighed. He wasn't in love with Anastasia, at least not anymore, but he just couldn't let her go, either. She was all he had. What would he be without her?

You are such a fool, Shiloh Leigdraca.

What magic had he cast, or forbidden knowledge had he read, that saddled him with the Voice? This mocking, cruel demon in his mind. Shiloh cradled his head in his hands, putting pressure on his temples to soothe his own madness.

You are not insane. I am not a curse, nor a demon. Your soul and mine mingled at your birth. Listen to me, for once in your pitiful life, the Voice growled. *Don't dwell in confusion and self-pity. There are more important matters at hand.*

"Like what?"

Where is Luze?

Luze. Shiloh pushed to his feet in a rush. *Where had he gone?* The garden was empty. He'd been acting strangely in the garden. Something wasn't right. Shiloh took a deep breath.

"Think about this rationally. Where would Luze have gone?" The next step of their plan had been to search Elaine's workshops—again. They searched through her tools, through every workshop they found scattered across the city, at least once a month, but found nothing of use. Shiloh hoped they'd missed something. Luze must have left to begin the search.

The Voice seemed dissatisfied with Shiloh's conclusion, but didn't offer any other ideas. Shiloh rushed to the stairs by the gazebo and began the descent. Like their usual routine, he would start with the workshop at Creon's house and hope Luze was still there, waiting for him.

The trip from the garden to Creon's house, down the road from the main plaza, felt longer than usual. A strange, fiery hum pooled in his gut, leaving him jittery—a feeling he blamed on how strained his magic had become ever since he'd started using battle magic. It certainly wasn't because he was worried. He wouldn't worry over Luze. Couldn't. Like a string pulled taut, Shiloh continued forward, only halting when he arrived in front of Creon's house.

The stone house looked like any other in Haven—narrow and high with a sharp, angled roof, making the most out of the room available in the inner city, though, considering it was Creon's house, it was wider than most. The leaders of Haven always occupied this house. It was three stories, like its neighboring homes, which were shoved up against it, sharing walls as if the entire block were one giant building. A couple of stairs led up to the front door, which was made of a dark wood, engraved with sigils.

That door was wide open. Shiloh rushed forward, dread and hope coiling together. In an instant, he imagined a hundred terrible scenarios—*Luze bleeding and sprawled on the floor from a Hollow attack, his body broken beyond repair, flesh and gore.*

He clenched his fists, preparing for whatever he found. The front room was empty and completely untouched. The couches and rugs, blankets neatly folded, were the same as they always had been. Shiloh moved deeper into the house, heading to Elaine's workshop, which was on the third floor.

He climbed the stairs two at a time, desperation urging him forward. At the end of the hall, the workshop door was wide open, revealing the room in complete disarray. Shiloh slowed, creeping into the room.

Elaine's books lay in heaps on the floor, tossed without care. Some were open, pages crinkling against the cold stone. Drawers were open, various objects dumped on the floor. *What happened here?*

At the far end of the room, Shiloh noticed something new. A section of wall slid away, revealing stairs that trailed up in a sharp curve. *A secret passage!* He'd looked, but never found a passage in any of Elaine's workshops. *How much had he missed?*

Shiloh crept up the stairs, holding his breath, as he listened for signs of whoever had been here. At the top of the stairs, Shiloh found a small room with barely enough headspace for him to stand comfortably. The walls turned inward sharply, making him realize he must be in some sort of attic.

A window by the stairs and a moss-lantern on the ceiling gave enough light to see clearly.

In the corner of the room, a man hunched over a desk. Long black hair curtained him, obscuring his face and whatever held his interest on the desk, but Shiloh recognized his silhouette. *Luze.* Shiloh finally released his breath. *He'd found him. Luze was fine. Everything was fine.*

It's not fine.

"Luze." Shiloh wanted to stand beside him, to look at his face, to relieve the strange uneasiness still lingering. Why did he feel so panicked? He should search through Elaine's workshop, too. "I can't believe you found this room."

Where is Luze?

Shiloh ignored the Voice, shoving it down. He'd found Luze. Everything was fine. There was no need to worry anymore.

Shiloh turned his attention to the room. It smelled old and damp, with the distinct aroma of old leather and parchment. Ten identical porcelain dolls lined the left wall, sitting on a shelf. He stepped closer, picking one up and turning it over in his hand. The doll felt strange. It pulled at his magic like a hungry void. Without thinking, he dropped the doll, which thunked to the ground without shattering. That *thing* was no ordinary doll.

Shiloh stumbled back, eyes dragging across the lines of dolls. No, not dolls, but empty ghouls—shells that were brought to life with a soul, and then used for various purposes, but most often as warriors. The Court of Bones was once renowned for its ghoul army. *Had Elaine been considering the same thing to fight against the Hollows?*

He shook his head. Ghouls were a dark magic. Subjugating souls wasn't something he'd ever expect from Elaine, but what did he know? He didn't know what that woman was capable of. *How had she even gotten her hands on ghoul shells?* He rubbed a hand across his forehead. That didn't matter. It wouldn't help him now.

Shiloh continued to look around the room. On a bookshelf below the dolls, several trinkets sat, glittering in the dim light of a moss-lantern hung from the peak of the ceiling. He crouched down. Dust fluttered around him, motes drifting and catching the light.

A compass, a few stones, an engraved knife, and a small stained-glass bowl sat in front of the books. Shiloh's attention lingered on the compass. *A tracker?* He held the compass up, inspecting it, letting his magic tease at the edges of the object. It certainly was enchanted.

He flipped it over, instantly recognizing the sigils inscribed on the back—all for locating. He shoved the tracking compass in his pocket and stood with a sigh. The uneasy feeling never left him. Fire still pooled in his stomach, twisting like an angry snake of nausea and anxiety.

"What have you found over there?" Shiloh asked, finally moving to Luze's side.

Luze turned, a strange grin stretching across his features.

"Luze? What is it?"

Not Luze.

On the desk by Luze's hand, a dull and lifeless red crystal set in intricate metal hung from a thin chain. The amulet.

"I think I've found what you were searching for." Luze dangled the amulet from a finger. "This soul vessel?" Luze looked to Shiloh, who reached for the amulet, his eyes wide.

"You found it," Shiloh said.

Luze jerked his hand away from Shiloh's grasp, keeping the amulet out of reach. "I have." Stepping away from Shiloh, Luze swung, throwing the amulet on the ground, shattering the delicate crystal.

"What are you doing?!" A piece of the red crystal rolled across the floor and fell in a crack of the wood, disappearing and taking Shiloh's hopes of saving Anastasia with it.

"Oops?" Luze laughed cruelly. "*Tofaran.*" With that word, a purple mist swirled around Luze, and his appearance shifted. The illusion faded, leaving Athan standing where Luze once stood.

Not Luze. Not Luze. Where is he?! Find! the Voice roared, breaking through all his attempts to silence him, to remain calm. "Where is Luze? What have you done with him?"

"My brother? Now you pretend to care?" Athan scoffed, folding his arms across his chest as he regarded Shiloh with annoyance. "Lulu would be better off without you."

Shiloh held his head in his hands. The pounding, screaming monster in his mind would not relent. Blood thundered in his ears.

"How many years have you spent dragging him by your side while you obsess over some pathetic human girl? You can't even keep her safe—or the two unconscious children in your house. Do you know how easy it was to break into your little fountain home?" Athan's smile turned vicious, canines lengthening to monstrous points. "My brother is safe from you now. Don't bother looking for him."

What has he done to Luze? The Voice writhed, clawing its way to the surface, begging to be let out.

Shiloh wanted to succumb, but he was afraid. He didn't understand the Voice, feared it. Fire rushed to Shiloh's fingertips, and Athan laughed.

"What fun I'll have with you," he said. "It would be a shame to ruin Elaine's workshop, though, wouldn't it?" Athan lunged forward and the stone floor moved with him.

A stone pillar punched into Shiloh's stomach, launching him against the wall by the stairs and through the window. Air rushed to meet him. Glass dug into his skin, but Shiloh barely felt it. His magic moved of its own accord. Fire rushed around him in a warm, protective embrace. He'd never used a spell like that—didn't even know how—but he didn't have the time to think about it.

Shiloh hit the street and rolled, body still engulfed in that protective flame. *"Tell me, where is Luze?"* Shiloh shouted. He couldn't tell whether those words had been his own or whether they'd belonged to the Voice.

Athan laughed, hovering above him on his shadowy wings. "You are no match for me."

He knew it was true. Shiloh was still too close to burning. He hadn't recovered fully from opening the gate in Elaine's wards, fighting off the Hollows, and now this?

We must make him talk. We must. We will.

Shiloh trembled as he hurled wave after wave of fire into the air, chasing after Athan's darting form, until he dropped his hands. His fingertips burned, nearly numb with the sensation. Kneeling on the cold street, Shiloh glared up at Athan.

Malice glinted in Athan's eyes; with a snap of his fingers, stone shackles latched onto Shiloh's wrists and ankles, keeping him locked in place. Air whipped around him, tearing at his clothes and stealing his breath. The swirling wind picked up broken pieces of glass from the ground, which darted around Shiloh, slicing at his flesh. The temperature dropped dramatically as the wind sharpened, howling around him.

Shiloh struggled to breathe. *Luze.* The pounding of his heart echoed in his ears. He jerked at the restraints, flailing with panic as darkness clouded the edges of his vision. He gasped for air.

As his body went limp and his vision faded, the wind receded. The last thing Shiloh heard was Athan's uncharacteristic anger.

"You will never be good enough for him."

Athan was right. Everyone was better off without him, especially Luze. Ignoring the furious thrashing of the Voice, Shiloh let the bliss of unconsciousness take him.

CHAPTER 16

Lana

The desert was far too cold for the thin clothes and armor that Lana still wore. Her thoughts drifted to the half-remembered snippets of Anastasia's life. Anastasia lived an isolated life. She trained alone. Shiloh had been her only friend until Alix and Meredith showed up one day. Lana wrapped her arms tightly around herself, as the chill of the desert mirrored the cold isolation in her sister's past.

Alix hurried them along their path into the desert, where the soldiers had made camp. A roaring bonfire surprised Lana in the center of the camp, and she quickly warmed herself in its flickering light.

The soldiers huddled close to the fire. Two of the three were asleep. Remi sat quietly in the sand, his hand loose on his sheathed sword. His head swung toward them, quickly noticing Alix and Lana. Though a delicate man, his face revealed his hard-won battles. A scar slashed across his cheek and marred the left side of his face, disfiguring his ear. His scars and rough, patchy beard looked out of place on his otherwise gentle face.

"I see you've brought company. Wounded company." Remi's voice was sweet, like the tinkling of a silver bell.

Alix nodded. "We're killing the beasts, and she's trying to rescue one."

He laughed.

Lana shivered at the sound, delightfully beautiful. It set her on edge. Alix didn't feel so foreign—so fae—but Remi did. Remi was like the stars and moonlight on a sea of blood. Beautiful and terrifying.

"Come here," he said to Lana, but she hesitated, taking a single stumbling step towards the strange fae.

Alix urged her forward. "Remi is our medic."

He smiled up at Lana and patted the sand at his side before pulling a satchel from a pile of nearby blankets. She sat down and let him inspect her wound, which had stopped dripping blood a while ago.

"What about the Hollows?" Lana asked. "Should we be out in the open like this?"

Alix's eyes scanned the horizon.Before them, only empty sands stretched in silence, while the vast abyss of the night sky glowed above them with glittering stars. Wind pulled at Alix's ponytail, whipping the strands across her face. "The pack doesn't roam this part of the desert at night, though we should wake well before sunrise to avoid the beasts as they seek refuge from the sun in Haven."

"What are your orders?" Remi asked, while carefully cleaning away the dried blood and debris from Lana's wound.

"An hour before dawn," she said, "we will enter Haven again and follow the trail of blood to their den, where we will wait. We will strike at the height of day, when they are at their weakest."

Remi nodded, and they fell silent again as he continued to tend to Lana.

"The wound has closed. Did you cauterize it?" He asked with a furrowed brow.

"No?" Had she? Lana frowned and reached to touch the wound, but Remi brushed her fingers away before she could touch her torn flesh.

Alix leaned over, looking at the wound. "Anastasia used to burn off her wounds mid-battle, but then we always had Mere..." She turned her back to them, focusing on the darkness of the desert sands.

"Right. Infection risk is a consideration," Remi said, inspecting the slashes on Lana's face. "Then I'll need to heal it properly."

Alix stiffened. Her gait was tight and forced as she walked to the other side of the camp. Lana raised her brows, watching the woman sit alone and stare into the desert.

"She's not fond of magic," Remi whispered. "Spending so much time fighting the Hollows, I find it worth the risk to heal our wounds." He shrugged. "You'll be useless to us if you fall into a fever and the rot that clings to the Hollows makes infection a near certainty. Will you let me?"

Lana glanced at Alix before nodding once. She hated letting someone take care of her, but what choice did she have? Alix was counting on her to fight the Hollows at her side with Anastasia's magic.

Remi's hands hovered over her face before a red mist floated between his fingers. Her skin tingled at first, but soon pain tore through her. Lana's wound reopened and sealed, smoothing over. Her agony was over almost as quickly as it had begun. The red mist sank into her skin, leaving her feeling feverish for a moment before Remi dropped his hand.

He offered her a tired smile. "You should get some sleep," he said, and then joined Alix at the far end of the camp, where they talked in conspiratorial whispers, sometimes fervent and sometimes resigned.

Alone, Lana sat on the sand, pulling her knees to her chest and wrapping her arms around them. When the Hollow attacked, if she hadn't jumped in front of Vas, maybe she could have done something different...used the flames again. Every time he was in danger, she jumped in the way. Maybe that was how she and Anastasia were alike—both recklessly self-sacrificing. If she could just take a minute to think, she'd find a better way, but her emotions always rushed to the surface, despite how much Lana tried to shove them away in that lockbox of her mind.

She sighed. Alix would help her and everything would be fine. She just needed to follow her lead. The golden fire that Lana now recognized as Anastasia floated to the surface, and a jolt of fear rushed through Lana. She didn't want to go back to that dark place in her mind—the place she'd gone when Anastasia had taken over. The golden warmth embraced her, soothed her, and for just a moment, Lana relaxed. For just *that* moment, she felt whole. Sprawled in the sand by the fire, she finally fell asleep, unafraid of what nightmares may come.

Lana woke from a dreamless sleep and followed Alix back down to Haven.

Alix was right about the blood. When they reached the city below the garden, heavy drops of blood streaked the stone, already black and thick on the stone, staining the ground unnaturally. Lana had never seen much blood, and definitely not to this excess.

They followed the trail, though it diverged and twisted as Hollows took different paths, but they all seemed to head to the same place—the plaza. The city was quiet, and Lana had the feeling of eyes on her again. She wanted to crawl into the nearest hole and hide, but Anastasia bubbled beneath the surface. The warm glow reminded her of her quest. She was not alone, and with Anastasia, she had no reason to be afraid.

The trail led all the way to the city hall. The sound of their footsteps echoed in the city's silence, leaving Lana on edge. Only yesterday, this plaza had been full of her worst nightmares, crowding in every corner and perching on the rooftops. *Where were the Hollows now?*

The trail stopped abruptly in front of city hall. Alix halted the small company of soldiers and scanned the area. They had moved carefully, stuck to the shadows, but now they were in the open with nowhere to hide.

A large, dark shape dove from the top of nearby ruins. As it neared the ground, Lana recognized the shape. It was a crow. Lana shivered. It looked a lot like the bird that flew out of the bookstore. It circled over them in a wide arc before drifting to the ground.

Alix and the soldiers drew their weapons, watching the bird with skilled alertness. When it neared the ground, it shifted. Red vines crawled from its beak and wrapped around its body as feathers fell away.

In a theatrical display of the grotesque, a man stood before them. Athan.

Athan bowed, dipping low with his hands flung out to the side. When he rose, he wore a grin that stretched across his face. The pulsating red vines sank into his skin once again, visible like veins underneath thin, pale skin.

"Welcome! Welcome," he said. "I would invite you in for tea, but I believe I'm fresh out." He laughed as he spoke.

"What have they done with him?" Lana stepped forward, pulling her sword from its sheath with a trembling hand. Anastasia rose within her mind, lending the golden embrace of her strength.

"With whom, my dear?"

"My friend." She hesitated, unwilling to say his name. She didn't trust this man.

"I'm sure you have a great deal of friends." He gestured to her sword. "Do you mean this one?" He twirled his hand, and a great expanse of purple fog coalesced in the air beside him. Images moved and sharpened until she could see figures. Liam slumped against a wall; ropes bound his legs and hands. "Or perhaps this one?" he asked with a cackle as the images changed and instead of Liam, Lana now saw Vas bound in the same way Liam had been.

Bile rose in Lana's throat. *Liam had been safe. He was asleep in Shiloh's house.* "How?" *How had Athan kidnapped him? Had he?* This must be some trick.

"No place in this city is beyond me. I'll gladly take you to them." He grinned.

"What's the catch?" Lana asked. Even if she were stepping into Athan's trap, she couldn't risk leaving Vas and Liam in the den. She wouldn't abandon them.

"You don't have to make deals with this wretch," Alix hissed, lunging toward Athan with her sword.

He stepped out of the way, moving with unnatural ease, like clouds or mist on the wind.

Alix followed his movements, circling around him with her sword.

"You're quite feisty. I don't think we've officially met, have we?" Athan dodged every lunge.

Lana watched. Several times, Alix's sword sliced at his arms and should have left deep cuts in his flesh, but her blade never marked him.

Alix growled in frustration.

"I'll take that as a no." He laughed again. "I don't suppose you've ever fought with a mage, hm?" His eyes were alight with a cat's delight.

Alix shifted her weight back, taking the sword in both hands and balancing it just over her shoulder. She didn't answer him. Remi watched with a predatorial gaze. Anastasia's memories mingled with Lana's thoughts. Remi had trained alongside Alix, fought with Alix since youth. They had ways of communicating in battle that were subtle and deadly, so when Alix had shifted her stance, Remi had shifted as well.

He moved with delicate stealth, inching closer toward Athan. His wicked sword, thin and sharp, pointed toward his heart.

"Perhaps we should end this little dance and get to the matter at hand, yes?" Athan turned suddenly away from Alix. The nails of his hand elongated as his claw wrapped around Remi's throat, and he gasped at the unexpected grapple.

Even so, Remi plunged the sword into Athan's chest, pushing it until it broke through on the other side. Athan slumped forward, leaning heavily into Remi, who, despite the sudden weight of him, seemed unfazed.

Remi pushed at his shoulders. But he wouldn't move. His hand slid into his flesh, disappearing. He yanked his hand back, and it came away clean.

Laughter bubbled up from Athan as he melted into a pool of bright red on the floor.

Remi stumbled back, shaking his sword free of the red liquid.

"That was lovely!" Athan yelled as he stepped out from the shadows near the city hall. "Such drama. Every delightful tale ends in tragedy. Beautiful." He giggled.

"It was an illusion," Lana said slowly, putting together the pieces of his unnatural movement and impossible dodges.

"Of course. I am a mage. Let us leave behind our play for now and get to the reason you're here."

Alix lunged toward him again with her blade.

Wings of red-veined smoke burst from his back, and he took to the sky, narrowly avoiding her swipe. "Ah. Ah. Play nice. I'd hate to ruin you." He smiled. There was a hungry look in his eyes, which were now red as fresh blood.

"What do you want?" Lana asked.

Athan pressed a hand to his chest and feigned offense. "What do I want? Oh no, my dear. I am only a servant in this endeavor. What is it you want?"

"I want my friends back. Where are they?"

"As I said, I'll take you to them, but only you and your feisty general."

"Why?" *What was he scheming?* He couldn't truly be planning to lead her straight to Vas and Liam, then let her leave.

"There's someone who would very much like to see the general, and I'll enjoy the drama," he said with another mad laugh.

Lana looked back toward Alix, who nodded. Remi protested quietly, but Alix just held up her hand, commanding his silence.

"All right," Lana said.

"Too quick to agree," he said. "I have one condition."

"What is it?"

"You must not interfere with matters between the Hollows and me. If a spat breaks out, ignore it. You are not to harm anyone. If either of you interferes, then our momentary truce is over. Otherwise, I'll make sure you leave unharmed."

Lana furrowed her brows and once again looked back toward Alix, who seemed similarly confused. *Why would either of them care what he did with the Hollows?*

"I accept your deal," she said.

Athan smiled. "Wonderful." With a muttered word, a magic wall of dancing shadow and shimmering light slammed down behind Alix and Lana, cutting them off from Remi and the other soldiers.

Lana pressed her hand back into the shadow, and it was soft, nothingness, like clouds.

Athan laughed at her prodding. "More illusions, yes. You found me again. It's a privacy screen. Come now, you two. Unless you want the others following us into depths where they are sure to be killed?" Athan looked pointedly at Alix as he finished speaking.

She shifted forward, moving to follow him. Her sword was sheathed, but her hand never left the hilt.

Lana followed, and the shadow drifted after them, spreading out into the plaza. With a sinister grin, Athan led them into the Hollows' den.

Light filtered in from above as they descended the staircase. Long before the light should have vanished, Athan's illusory shadow slipped in, covering the staircase and blocking the remaining light.

The tunnel went deep underground, surprising Lana, considering Haven itself was already underground. She wasn't afraid—mostly—of the darkness or the cold damp of the ground, but she wasn't particularly fond of it either.

Though the staircase was dark, Athan continued. His footsteps echoed on the walls and rang out confidently, not missing a step. Athan's and her own were the only footsteps she could hear; worrying Alix had disappeared, Lana reached out in front of her. Her hand met the worn metal of Alix's armor and she was relieved. Straining to hear, the sound of Alix's breathing became apparent. Quiet, inhale and exhale. Almost nonexistent.

Her stealth suddenly struck Lana. A predator in the dark. Lana held on, grasping a strap that ran across Alix's back. Despite that, Lana still stumbled a few times on her way down. The stairs were mostly even, but she didn't expect the gentle curves that sometimes appeared.

The stairs ended on flat ground. Lana reached a hand out to the side, feeling for the walls. Her fingertips brushed against cold, moist walls that were cracked and craggy, rough like raw rock. She drew her hand back immediately, wiping the moisture from her fingers onto her pants. The tunnel was still dark, but as they continued, the darkness lightened.

There was a light at the end of the hallway, warm and yellow. Lana's heart jumped at the promise of light. She didn't understand why he had agreed to bring her down to the Hollows. Lana didn't know where they were going. She certainly shouldn't trust him to keep her safe—of course. She had Alix and Anastasia, so she was as safe here as anywhere else.

Her grip tightened on Alix's strap. *Who was he bringing them to meet? Would he bring her to Liam and Vas first?*

At the end of the hallway, Athan didn't hesitate as he stepped into the room full of light.

The room had no corners, just smooth curved walls in a large oval. There were a few openings that led off to other dark hallways in various directions. The room contained sparse furnishing. Tattered and stained rugs littered the floor.

In the center of the room, a fire crackled. A large kettle hung above the firepit, bubbling with some strange liquid. Smoke lifted steadily from the fire, drifting up toward the ceiling, where cracks opened in the stone. Lana watched the tendrils of smoke dive into the dark crevices until Athan's voice broke into her thoughts.

"Welcome to the queen's den," he said with a flourish of his hand. "You should consider yourself lucky, honored even, that you are guests here."

"Where are the winged Hollows? Where are my friends?" Lana asked.

"Not far from here. We'll get there, I assure you." Athan smiled a snake's smile. "But first, your part of the bargain. Rest here. I'll be back."

Before Lana could say anything, Athan disappeared in a whirl of smoke that obscured the hallways nearby. She was certain he had slipped down one of them, but he had made sure she wouldn't know which one.

CHAPTER 17

Alix

Lana paced. Alix stood still and silent, watching her as she walked back and forth, nearly tripping over knots in the rugs at her feet. Eventually, Lana gave up and sat on the floor, staring into the darkness of the hallways that led away from the room.

"Why are we waiting?" Lana asked.

What other option did they have? The weight of eyes lurked in every shadow. Alix had counted every turn, memorized the path even in the dark. The map in her mind's eye put them deep underground, deeper than she knew possible. At that moment, they waited in the den of her enemy.

Alix controlled each breath and spoke with quiet authority to the mousy girl inhabiting her friend's body. "You wait because you're afraid. I wait because we're outnumbered."

Lana protested, "Hey. Wait. No. I'm not afraid. I came down here to save Vas."

"Did you?" Alix raised her brows.

"Of course I did." Lana crossed her arms, hugging herself tight as she glared into the dark hallway. Alix couldn't help but notice the similarities between Lana and her sister. The way her eyes narrowed and the cadence of her voice all reminded her painfully of the friend who had abandoned her to become an ineffectual martyr.

Alix sighed, rolling her shoulders. "Untested warriors are full of bravery until bravery is required."

Lana grimaced. "Do you hate me? Because you don't seem to be too happy with me."

Hate her? She didn't know Lana, but Anastasia? Alix stretched her arms. Had she grown to hate her friend? "Most would tell you I'm always this rough."

"That's not true," Lana said, her voice quiet.

Alix raised her brows. "And you would know."

"Anastasia showed me. I've been in her memories. I've seen you. I know you, and this isn't you." The fire flickered from a gentle breeze drifting down the dark hallways. An unexpected rage flashed through Alix. Shiloh would be held accountable for the mess he'd made of Anastasia. She would make him pay in blood. Anastasia had been resting from this blasted eternal war between fae and Hollow. What was the point? The fury rushed away, leaving Alix with the heaviness of her past.

The fighting would never end. Why must she continue? Twenty-five years of bloodshed weighed on her heart with a sinking nausea. Nothing had changed in all these years. What use was she? Worthless. Without Meredith, what did this life matter? *Meredith.*

A sharp pain singed up her spin, and she took a sharp breath. The last time she'd seen her fated mate rushed, unbidden, to her thoughts. She desperately tried to force the memories away, but it was no use.

"Choose me, Alix. Believe me." Meredith dug her hands into her hair, twisting strands painfully tight around her long fingers.

"Choose you?" Alix scoffed. "When have you ever chosen me?"

"Wha–" Meredith began, but Alix cut her off with terse words spat through clenched teeth.

"It has always been about magic, and now these monsters. You have chosen your obsessions over your mate." The heat of the dying desert sun surrounded them. Not even the promise of the night's cool touch could soothe Alix.

Meredith pulled her hair taut and glared at Alix. "I chose you when I used *magic* to save your father. I chose you when

I killed Hollows at your side. I killed them, Alix. Don't you understand what that meant to me? I've chosen you, but I can't keep slaughtering them anymore." She bared her teeth, showing canines sharper than they'd ever been before.

Alix faltered, caught by that subtle change she didn't understand. Her heart hammered in her chest, but she refused to let her mate continue this way. Why couldn't Meredith see how stupid she was being? "You won't slaughter them? They've brutalized people we know — people we love. Or did you not care when—"

"You don't understand!" Meredith's voice — hoarse and sharp — wailed over the strengthening wind. "Those fae aren't dying. They're turning. There's just something wrong with some of them."

"With some of them?" Jagged heat tore through Alix's stomach, twisting her insides in knots. "All of them are feral, bloodthirsty beasts."

Meredith shook her head, closing her eyes tight. "No. I can hear them, Alix. I can hear all of them now." Meredith fell to her knees, clutching her head against her chest. Red magic pulsed around her. "I can hear every single one of their voices." Meredith choked out the words as the magic exploded around her.

Shadows rose and consumed Meredith.

She was gone.

Lost.

And Alix was alone.

"Alix?" Lana asked. Wrinkles creased her forehead and her pursed lips. "What's wrong? Why are you acting like this?" she repeated her question.

Alix inhaled, clenching her fists as she chased away the lingering memories. "People change," she whispered.

"I guess so. No one is the same as they were in Anastasia's memories," Lana said, crossing her arms.

"That is true, but you're right." Alix straightened her breastplate as she whispered. "I am angry. Not at you. Well, not entirely. So perhaps you're right and this isn't me."

"I don't understand."

"Shiloh shouldn't have meddled where he did. This," she gestured to Lana, "isn't what Anastasia would have wanted. She chose to be put in magical stasis—to sacrifice her conscious life for the good of her people." No matter how much it had hurt Alix when her friend abandoned her, she respected her decision.

"Elaine and Shiloh never cared about what she wanted. Anastasia always wanted to be a hero. She actually cared about the humans *and* the fae. What they did…" Ana had slept through the last two decades of blood and pain, and now she was being forced to return to this endless battle. It wasn't right. Alix crossed her arms, glaring at the fire. Silence stretched between them as Alix continued to stare into the undulating flames.

She shook her head, clicking her tongue in irritation. "Anastasia wouldn't have wanted that, and now here you are, forcing her to wake from her hero's slumber. Maybe I am upset—she knows now what was done to her by the people she loved most. Betrayal hurts."

"Oh," Lana said. Still sitting on the cold floor, away from the fire, Lana drew herself up, pulling her knees to her chest.

Alix pursed her lips. A better person would comfort Lana, but what was she to say? That Anastasia's awakening wasn't her fault? That everything would be okay? Nothing was okay and Alix didn't believe life would ever be okay again. She avoided looking at Lana and instead settled into a silent watchfulness.

It was still some time later before Athan returned and led them down a hallway lit with dim torches of blue mosslight. They took exactly 4 turns where the path forked off. Right. Left. Right. Right. Alix added the new directions to her mental map of the Hollow's den.

At the end of their journey, a room opened up that was almost identical to the last, but at the back of the room sat an enormous patchwork throne. Pillows and rugs piled high, forming the couch-like throne.

Upon the throne, a Hollow woman, with short black hair, sat. Though soft shadows wreathed her body and red vines crawled along her arms, she was regal and delicate. She wore familiar armored skirts that stopped just at her knees, revealing the chainmail leggings she wore underneath. Metal lace adorned her bodice and flared down onto the skirt. Her gloved hands were delicate, perfect for the rapier that swung at her hip, though, with a tightness in her chest, Alix didn't miss the weightier, double-headed axe that rested carefully at her back, covered with a thick leather to avoid accidental injury. Even sitting down, it was obvious how tall she was. This woman was imposing, frightening. Alix's mouth opened and her heart threatened to leap from her chest as she fully took in the woman she knew better than her own reflection.

Alix knew the way her breath felt against skin and the taste of her smile. She clenched her fists, struggling against the urge to fall at her feet. Alix had waited for this day for twenty-five years and had dreamed of the moment she would see her again.

This wasn't what she had expected. Athan brought them to the feet of the Hollow queen. Though she was marred by time and the putrid shadows of the Hollows, Alix would recognize her mate anywhere.

"Meredith," Alix breathed her name like a prayer. Her breath caught and her throat tightened. Water dripped audibly from the stone ceiling, punctuating the stillness as the two women regarded each other.

The Hollow queen stood. The mosslight caressed her ethereal face. Her red eyes, trained on Alix, only slightly widened, betraying her surprise.

The queen spoke in the same unintelligible tones as she did when addressing the Hollows on the rooftop. Alix furrowed her brows. The sounds blended and merged until the meaning unfolded in her mind.

"Alix." A hint of a smile played in the corners of Meredith's mouth. "Have you come to kill me as you once promised?"

Alix took a halting step toward her. Her tongue darted across chapped lips. This was it. She had to draw her sword. The only way to free Mere from the curse was death. Her fingers shook as Alix wrapped them around the hilt.

Meredith stepped forward, meeting Alix. Though she was barely an inch taller than Alix, Meredith looked down at her intensely while Alix gazed up with a mix of fierceness and longing, her fingers clasping and unclasping on the hilt of her sword. A single strike and it would be over. The image of Meredith's crumpled body, bleeding out on the floor, flashed through Alix's mind. Bile rose to the back of her throat.

"I would like to remind you, General, attacking anyone while in our home would violate our agreement." Athan stood near the forking tunnels, watching with a curious glint in his eyes.

Alix's shoulders sagged, and she let out a ragged breath. "Right." She stepped back, turning away from the queen of the Hollows. "Then let us get on with our task."

"Wonderful," Athan said.

"If not to kill me, why are you here?" Meredith asked, now speaking in the common language of the fae. Meredith lingered by Alix's side. The sound of her voice, without the screeching tones of Hollow-speak, vibrated through Alix. If she closed her eyes, could she pretend the last two decades hadn't happened?

"To find my friends," Lana said, shattering Alix's brief illusion.

Meredith glanced toward Lana for the first time, and her eyes truly widened. "Anastasia, you're awake?"

Alix shook her head. "It's complicated. That's Lana, Elaine's other daughter."

Meredith rested an elegant finger against her neck as she looked between Lana and Alix. "Hmmm. I suppose I should have been keeping a closer eye on Shiloh." She tossed an imperious glance at Athan. "What friend of hers could I possibly have in my home?"

Athan waved his hand dismissively. "A boy brought in from the garden."

Meredith's eyes grew distant for a moment before she nodded. Immediately, Alix recognized that expression. She was hiding something. "Of course. I should accompany you for this guest." What did Mere know?

Athan tapped a finger to the small smile on his lips. "As I had hoped, my queen."

Her eyes narrowed on Athan, but she didn't respond, merely waited with her arms crossed.

Athan gestured toward a small door at the back of the throne room. So once again, Alix followed Athan into another dark hallway.

"He's not far, I promise," Athan said. "He has his own quarters in the guest wing and guards for protection."

"I thought Hollows ate people," Lana said.

Meredith's tinkling laugh bounced around the hallway, each one stabbing through Alix's resolve. How did she ever think herself capable of freeing Meredith from this curse?

"We eat magic, not people," Meredith said.

Years of slaughter rose in her troubled mind. The Hollows did more than consume magic. She grit her teeth. "Lies," Alix growled. "Your beasts tear us apart and drink the blood from the ground."

"Us?" Meredith scoffed. "*You* are us, Alix. Fae aren't so fragile to die from a little blood loss." She exhaled sharply. "We will live in harmony, as the ancients once did."

A hissing sound rose from the darkness in the distance, and Meredith bared her teeth toward the unknown.

Alix's hand went to the hilt of her sword. "Something's not right."

"Everything is perfectly fine," Athan assured as he hurried them along, across another open room and down a hallway.

Shallow comforts from the lips of a traitor. Alix readied herself. She wouldn't be caught off guard a second time.

CHAPTER 18

Lana

The hallway was much wider than the rest, and even with moss-torches hanging on the right wall nearby, the dimness remained. Shadows danced in the recesses of the rock. Lana shivered and wrapped her arms around herself.

Something tapped in the shadows, scurrying across the rock and slipping out of sight. Lana glanced over her shoulder, but couldn't see anything. The hallway behind them had gone completely dark. The torches dimmed into darkness each time they passed. Why would Athan be using magic on the torches? What was he hiding? She couldn't see anything, but thought she caught the gleam of eyes as the last torch went out and they stepped into another round room.

This room was full of doors. Two humanoid Hollows stood in front of a nearby door. Athan gestured to the guards, and they stepped aside, allowing him to open the door.

Liam slumped in the center of a mattress of blankets and pillows. And Vas sat in the corner, with bandages wrapped across his chest and shoulders. The sight of them in the dirty cave room made her heart echo in her ears as she grit her teeth. They shouldn't be stuck in a dank room beneath the city. Neither wore any ropes or bindings, despite what Athan had shown her only hours ago in the plaza. But that didn't calm her. Lana took a deep breath, exhaling forcefully.

Vas turned slowly toward the door as it opened, his lips already poised for a snarl. After his eyes met Lana's, the aggression left him and was replaced with confusion as he looked between Lana and Alix.

"We're leaving," she said, trying to sound gentle and comforting as she offered her hand to help Vas stand, but felt the roughness of her words as they left her lips. She would have to carry Liam. In Anastasia's body, she felt confident she could.

Vas took Lana's hand, squeezing it for a moment before letting her help him up. The soft warmth of his palm soothed her raging emotions for a moment. Lana pulled her hand away, reminding herself that the strange comfort he brought was because of Anastasia. Her sister knew this fae and cared for him. That was the only reason she wanted to sigh in relief when she saw him. That was the only reason his presence was like cool water smothering the flames of her ire. It had to be.

Her only friend slumped in the corner. For him, she once again pushed away the strange thoughts. Lana dropped beside Liam. Unconscious, but breathing. No injuries. Perfectly fine, but asleep. Lana placed her hand against his cheek as she whispered apologies. He wouldn't be here if it weren't for her. *All her fault*. The words wrapped around her heart and squeezed.

"He's just letting us go?" Vas asked.

"That's what he said," Lana replied.

"But he's the reason I'm here. Athan is up to something."

"Oh, you are quite right, my prince. I never said I'd let you go, yet," Athan said. "My deal was with you, Keeper. I'd lead you to your friend and let you leave unharmed. Only you. You've served your purpose when you brought the general." His eager eyes turned to Alix. "How do you think it will feel to die on the fangs of the creatures you have hunted? All those you've killed—thwarting my plans—will be avenged."

Alix stood quietly nearby, her hand tight on the hilt of her sword. She was the first to see the Hollows slinking into the room from every hallway, surrounding them. Alix pulled her sword from its sheath, brandishing it toward the Hollows.

"You knew about this ambush," Alix said, turning an accusing eye to Meredith, who shook her head.

"No..." Meredith lifted her chin, narrowing her eyes at Athan with the authority of a noblewoman. "Athan, what are you doing? You told me explicitly that you'd release the prince."

Athan turned and addressed the creatures in the shadows. "See how weak your queen is? How easily she lets her guard down around the enemy? She wants you to live alongside those who hate you. But I know we can be far more. We can rule! Why should we ever bow to the whims of those beneath us who refuse to accept their true nature?!"

The Hollows screeched in response, cheering Athan's words. They circled closer, hungry eyes trained on Alix, Meredith, Lana, and Vas.

Meredith commanded them in that foreign tongue, but the Hollows didn't back away. They continued stalking into the room, pressing further upon them. "The Silvid's hate is merely fear. If we banish the fear, the hate dies!" She cried out over the gnashing teeth of the Hollow horde.

Laughter bubbled from Athan, a bright, hysteric laughter. Athan raised his hands in greeting, wiggling his fingers. "How naïve your queen is. Fear will let *us* rule." Athan stepped forward with a menacing smile. "Take what belongs to you, creatures of shadow!" Athan yelled.

The Hollows lunged forward in a mass, converging on Meredith, but she was strong and quick. Her sword cut through them and tossed them aside. When her sword failed, Meredith pulled the heavy axe from her back and swung it with more strength than Lana had imagined the delicate Hollow could have. In an instant, Alix was also in the fray, fighting off creatures that fell upon her with rabid snarls and open mouths.

Distracted by the chaos, Lana almost missed Athan dragging Vas into a corner and holding him down with magically manipulated shackles of stone. She yelped as the ground moved beneath her feet, where she still crouched beside Liam's unconscious body. The stone moved and pulled them to Athan.

"I do love an audience," Athan said. The stone shifted again, slithering up Lana's body and restraining her. "You get to watch as I restore the prince to his rightful power. Those idiots in the Silvid Court couldn't appreciate him."

Vas and Lana struggled against the stone, but without Silvid magic, they were trapped. Athan wrapped his fingers delicately around Liam's upper arms and pulled Liam toward him. Brandishing a dagger carved with symbols and set with gems, he cut a bright-red slash down Liam's arm.

"Leave him alone!" Lana threw herself against the stone, desperate to break free.

"I'm sorry, my prince, this may hurt just a moment, but I promise it will be worth it." Ignoring her pleas, Athan slashed an identical cut down Vas's arm, pulling a hiss of pain from his lips. "This tool is such a marvel. Lucky for me, I happened to find Elaine's secret workshop. It was full of such interesting things. I had no hope of fixing my changeling prince before this trinket."

"Changeling?" Vas slumped against the rock. "I'm not a changeling. I was born here. I'm a fae." He furrowed his brows, struggling to understand.

"Born here the first time, yes, but the second?" Athan gestured to Liam's limp body. "Not quite. Though I never expected the wellspring would send your soul to the mundane world. If only I'd realized sooner..." Athan frowned, then picked up Liam's bleeding arm and shoved it against Vas's, forcing their blood to mingle.

Golden magic exploded, and Vas screamed. The light blinded Lana. Only the sounds of the Hollows fighting behind them and the cold stone pressed to her skin kept Lana grounded against the fear that threatened to overwhelm her. Within her, Lana felt something shift. Anastasia writhed beneath the surface, a turmoil of emotions that Lana didn't understand.

The light died away, and Athan held the dagger high above Liam's heart. "The strange thing about changelings — if there are two bodies, the soul stretches itself thin, ballooning back and forth between bodies."

Lana strained against the stone bindings holding her still. What was Athan planning to do? "Let him go!" As her heart pounded, magic surged in her veins, burning and screaming for release, with each thunderous beat.

Athan continued talking, ignoring her struggles. "The prince can never be whole, can never reach his potential with this drain on his soul. So, there's one way to fix that."

Athan swung the dagger toward Liam's heart.

But before the dagger could split his flesh, the energy writhing beneath Lana's skin exploded as she screamed. Fire shot from her, charging at Athan with an intense, unnatural heat. The stone burned away from her wrists, freeing her from the shackles Athan had created.

The fire enveloped Athan and he scrambled away, clawing at the flames that licked his flesh. "How dare you interfere," he growled. Lana rushed forward, fire still sizzling on her skin, but Athan easily backstepped each of her clumsy attacks. She wouldn't let him hurt Liam.

With an easy grace, Athan released the stone prison around Vas and picked him up. Even with an unconscious Vas in his arms, cradled against his chest like a child, Athan dodged every spark of fire Lana shot. He stomped and the stone leapt up, smashing against the back of her knees and making her fall to the ground. The fire died from her skin, and her energy left with it. She slumped forward, struggling to catch her breath. The golden light of Anastasia's soul trembled with exhaustion from the unexpected burst of magic. *It's too much,* Anastasia whispered. *My soul is too shattered for this much magic.*

Using a gust of wind, Athan retrieved the changeling dagger. "I don't need to kill the boy." He gestured with his head to the Hollows that still surrounded her and her friends. "As long as he dies, the prince will be free. The beasts can handle that for me." He grinned, sharp canines pressing against his bottom lip. "I have better things to do."

As Lana, bloody and bruised, crawled toward Liam's unconscious body, Athan walked away with Vas.

CHAPTER 19

Lana

The remaining Hollows in the room closed in on Alix, Lana, and Meredith. The weakest, slowest Hollows attacked first, fueled by a hungry frenzy. Alix, already drenched in their putrid blood, swung her sword, cleaving into their flesh, which fell away like rot, revealing muscle and bone. Black blood fell to the floor in old, clotted chunks.

Seeing Alix, Lana pulled the sword from its sheath, desperately hoping Anastasia would surface soon. She reached inside herself, seeking that golden glow, but fear swallowed her whole. The flicker of Anastasia's familiar guidance rose to the surface for a moment before Lana's panic washed her away. All the emotions that she'd tried so hard to ignore since arriving in Kaelum rushed to the surface, blinding Lana from all else.

She held the sword in front of her as she struggled with herself. She was a target that a few Hollows noticed. They sprung from the shadows, eager to dig their claws and teeth into her flesh.

Alix rushed toward her and fought the Hollows off, keeping them at bay, but Alix's sword wavered with exhaustion.

And Lana was useless. She looked on at the scene before her. Dead creatures littered the floor, now slick with blood. Meredith fought with sword and claw, red vines lashing out and throwing Hollows to the ground.

Alix shielded Lana, who still sat on the ground, useless. The Hollows outnumbered them. This fight would end with death, and Lana was certain that death would be her own.

As Alix continued to fight off the attacks from the Hollows, an emptiness slithered through Lana's body. Her shoulders slumped. She should have left Feyville when Liam had asked her. She would be safe, starting a new life in a city with her best friend, struggling with her long-standing feelings for him she'd always ignored and now, even if she admitted the truth to herself, it didn't matter. She couldn't tell Liam how she felt. He and Vas were the same soul, and Vas was in love with her sister. It was all too complicated.

Instead, she was in a dank cave, underneath a desert that reeked of dead things. She was going to die here. Anastasia would die with her. A sob caught in her throat, and she pushed herself up to her feet. She didn't want her only sister to die in the dark with her, a simpering coward.

If only she could be more like Anastasia.

Lana held the sword up above her head as she stepped out into the sea of Hollows. Her hands still shook, but she brought the sword down on the back of a nearby Hollow. The sword bit into flesh, cutting through like moldy butter.

Lana gagged as she stumbled back, watching the black blood fall to the floor. The Hollow screeched and its eyes locked onto her. It lunged forward, but Alix twisted just in time, cleaving the head of the Hollow in one strong sweep.

The other Hollows hissed in outrage, but retreated away from the trio, fearful of Alix's eager blade.

Meredith glanced her way. It was a brief glance, but still a moment too long.

A rogue Hollow sank their wolf-like fangs into Meredith's shoulder, and tore back with a sudden rip, pulling flesh from bone. She roared, and the Hollows fell to the floor at the noise, whimpering and dragging themselves into the shadows at her fury.

Alix yelled and rushed forward, blade flashing. She launched herself toward the Hollow, but her attack didn't land. He dodged away, leaving her over-extended and full of fury. Meredith tried to move in front of her, but she wasn't quick enough. The Hollow's claws ripped across her side, piercing the weaknesses in her armor. Alix screamed in pain, blood pouring from her wound. She sank to the floor, pressing her hands into the torn flesh, trying to stanch the bleeding.

Meredith vibrated with shadowy magic as she lunged toward the Hollow. She was weak from the fight, but in her anger, she swatted the Hollow against the wall, where a sickening crack left it sliding down the wall in a limp, gruesome mess.

The few Hollows that had remained turned tail and fled, leaving the trio alone in the dark room with their injuries and the reek of Hollow blood.

CHAPTER 20

Vas

Vas suddenly woke from a dead sleep, gasping for breath. His arm stung where the changeling dagger had sliced him open. The stinging increased, burning as if a fire raged beneath his skin. He rubbed his hand over the wound and noticed the flesh was knitting back together. He writhed in an unfamiliar bed as the sting became an indescribable itching.

He felt his very soul stretching and thrumming. Images of an unfamiliar place, memories of a world without magic, flashed in his mind and disappeared, like waves lapping at a shore. Clawing at his skin, he thrashed until a strange warmth settled over him and swept him into a dream.

The dream was dark. Endless night and nothingness.

Except for a young man, a human, who sat on the flat void. The man, tall and lanky with dark messy curls, drew shapes on the ground with his fingers. Though his movements didn't leave any marks on the void.

"Hello?" Vas asked, approaching him.

The man's attention snapped to Vas. With a relieved grin, the man pushed himself to his feet. "Finally, someone else. We've got to get out of here. I need to find Lana." As he stepped forward, his eyes raked across Vas, lingering on his horns. He then furrowed his brow, which framed his bright green eyes. "Unless you're the reason I'm stuck here. Who are you?"

"Stuck?" Vas stared into the empty black of the dream. "I fell asleep." He shook his head. It was just a dream. When he woke, he had actual problems to face. Vas stiffened. What if this was another of Athan's games? "Who are you?"

"I'm Liam. Who are you?" the man repeated, stretching up to his full height.

Liam. The name twisted in Vas's gut. His changeling. Lana's best friend. He relaxed a fraction. Athan wouldn't have any use for Liam, and certainly wouldn't want Vas to meet him, considering Athan wanted Liam dead. To his former teacher, Liam was an obstacle to be solved. Something he'd shown in the Hollow den. If Lana hadn't exploded with magic, Liam would be dead, but his changeling still lived as far as Vas knew. The mark of Athan's magic dagger must have opened the connection between the halves of their soul.

Which meant this might not be an ordinary dream, but one shared between the pieces of his soul —- a place where Liam and Vas could truly speak.

"I'm Vasileios, but you can call me Vas." He rubbed his knuckles along his jawline. "I think we have a lot to talk about."

"Where's Lana?"

Vas sat down on the void, crossing his legs and leaning back on his palms. "She's with the two strongest knights I've ever known, so she's safe." And if she wasn't, Vas felt certain he would feel it in the thin thread that connected his soul and hers — the bond. He still wasn't sure which woman's soul he was bound to, but either way he knew his mate was safe.

Liam visibly relaxed and slumped down on the ground near Vas. "So then, let's talk. Where are we? There were these rotting wolf beasts and then a portal. And what are you?"

Vas settled in to explain everything to his changeling. He told him of the faerie world and the Hollows, which only seemed to confuse Liam. Then he told him of their joined souls.

"So, we're the same person?" Liam blinked heavily. "This is absolute nonsense. Fairies and monsters. No."

"We're the same soul, yes. Though, I suppose we share it, which explains why you've been in a coma since entering Kaelum."

Liam flopped backward onto the ground. "I'm in a coma. Yes. That makes sense. This is all a strange dream."

"Maybe it is, but what if it's not?"

Liam craned his neck to look at Vas. "What do you mean?"

"What will you do if it's not a dream?"

Liam dropped his head back to the ground and squinted at the darkness. "I'll do whatever I have to keep Lana safe, to bring her back home."

Vas's heart clenched at the thought of Lana leaving his side, but Liam was right. She deserved to be home, away from the danger of the faerie realm.

"Good," Vas said. Then, he stretched out on the ground beside Liam.

Together, they stared into the void in silence, waiting for the dream to end.

CHAPTER 21

Lana

Lana curled up on the ground, pressing her forehead into the stone. Her carefully braided hair was in tatters around her, making a curtain that hid her face, obscuring her self-loathing from the world.

She couldn't do anything right, and Anastasia was beyond her reach. A jumble of thoughts filled her mind, buzzing with emotions she refused to feel. That haze held her hostage, placing a barrier between Lana and Anastasia. Without Anastasia, she was helpless, and everything was hopeless. She lifted her head and remembered that she wasn't alone. Her best friend was still unconscious on the ground, and Alix was potentially bleeding out in the corner with Meredith.

Meredith. She had been one of Anastasia's friends too, and Alix's mate — a concept that Anastasia had understood no better than Lana did now, but Meredith had left. She had abandoned them and sided with the Hollows. Lana shook her head. The memories were too much for her and most of them still didn't quite make sense to her.

Lana pushed herself up and rushed over to where Liam sprawled on the ground. His breath was slow and even. He was fine. Lana brushed her fingers through his hair and her shoulders relaxed. Nearby, Alix reclined against the wall with Meredith's torso pulled into her lap.

They both looked gruesome, but Meredith was the worse of the two. She had slowly shifted back, letting go of the animalistic magic that had contorted her flesh. Once again, she looked completely like a normal fae, though mangled by her injuries.

Meredith spoke in that distorted way of the Hollows and Alix nodded, whispering softly as she brushed her fingers across the Hollow queen's cheek. Lana didn't know what to think of the scene—Alix, the enemy of the Hollows, gently cradling their queen, speaking with her in their language? Could Alix forgive Meredith so easily?

Ignoring her confusion for now, Lana assessed their situation. Blood dripped down Meredith's torn armor. Unlike the other Hollows, her blood was brighter, fresher, still warm and red—she wondered if that was why she didn't have that awful rotten flesh stench, like the others did. Broken bones were exposed on her right leg. Meredith needed help if she were to survive. Alix had a few deep cuts, hastily tied off with ripped fabric, but nothing was visibly broken. They both needed help. Lana's heart raced. She was the only one still standing and the only one left to do anything.

"What do I do?" Lana squeaked.

"Put up that sword, for one," Alix said. Her voice was a hoarse whisper.

Lana picked her sword up from the ground and sheathed it.

"We need to find Remi. He has our medical supplies. He is likely waiting for us outside, unless he and the knights circled around the den for another way in."

"I can't leave you here. What if the Hollows come back?"

Alix ran her fingers gently across Meredith's hair. "Then I'll fight until my dying breath. Go. Tell Remi." Alix leaned her head back, resting against the wall as her eyes fell closed in exhaustion.

Meredith's fingers twitched, and she lifted her hand, grasping Alix's fingers in her own.

"I don't even know where to go," Lana said.

"Four turns — Left, Left, Right Left. That will take you back to the first holding room, from there..."

Lana searched for paper for anything to write Alix's instructions. Nothing. The room was full of rancid flesh and blood. Lana grabbed a pillow from Meredith's throne and looked around with wide, frantic eyes.

Alix's jaw clenched and unclenched and she exhaled roughly. She looked down at Meredith, searching her face for an answer.

"I'm not so fragile anymore," Meredith said, her voice rough. "Look." She gestured to the red vines that snaked across her body. As moments passed, the vines stitched her flesh together, pulling bones back in place. "I could help you. I could heal your injuries, Alix, with magic." Through her pain, Meredith smiled up at Alix, sharp fangs pressing against her already bloody lips.

With her words, Alix stiffened and shook her head. "I can't. Don't use your magic, please."

Meredith searched Alix's face, a crease between her brows. When she spoke again, commanding, her expression was gentle. "We leave now." Her smile shifted to a determined sneer. "We cannot allow Athan to take the throne or put some puppet upon it. We're doing this together. I'm not letting you leave my side again, Alix." Meredith's hoarse voice dropped to a whisper in those last words.

Alix looked up toward Lana and the emotion drained from her face, leaving behind a wall, emotionless. Nothingness. "Then, we'll go together."

"I can go on my own," Lana said, though her voice was barely a squeak.

Alix just laughed coldly. "There's not enough pillows for you to write on to explain every turn to get out of this place and then to find Remi. Grab the boy and let's go."

Lana was hesitant, but she obeyed. Alix, still suffering from her own injuries, struggled under Meredith's weight, groaning in pain. Surprising herself with her own strength, Lana pulled Liam up and maneuvered him across her shoulders in a fireman's carry. For a moment, she felt the flicker of Anastasia's golden light slipping into her bones and supporting her arms as she followed Alix and Meredith down the hall.

With each step, Meredith gained her strength, until she was the one slowly leading them through the maze of the Hollows' den, walking on her own without their help.

"I don't understand," Lana whispered to Alix. "What's going on with you and Meredith?"

Alix's expression hardened. "There's nothing for you to understand."

"What happened to destroying the Hollows?" Lana chewed on her bottom lip. The Hollows were dangerous. Nowhere would be safe as long as they existed, but Meredith was Hollow now, wasn't she? She brought her fingertips to her lips, biting at the corner of a nail.

"I am—I will," she said, though the tremor in her words or the obvious affection in her eyes weren't convincing.

"Is this because she's your mate? I thought she rejected you?" Lana whispered, gesturing to Meredith, who had taken the lead a few paces ahead of them.

Alix gave her a sharp look, but didn't reply. She just continued to follow Meredith down the hallway, taking turns through the dark maze of the Hollows' den.

What was Lana missing? She bit her nail again, too deep, and blood welled at the surface. Had Alix been lying the entire time? Was she caught up in this? "You speak Hollow."

"The language isn't much different from Silvid," she said. "Any Silvid could understand it." Alix tossed her hand up in the air, dismissing the conversation. "I don't owe you an explanation. You nearly killed her, me, and the prince you were trying to rescue. I hoped you'd be more like Anastasia, but you're a coward. What are you so afraid of? Doesn't seem to be the Hollows, with the way you throw yourself into the fight unprepared."

Lana stammered, but fell silent. Her footsteps slowed, and she fell behind. Alix was right, after all. Lana had done nothing useful when the Hollows swarmed. She was the reason Vas was captured. She was useless. But she didn't want to be. Lana wanted to be brave. She wanted to be strong. She wanted to be the hero, but every time she tried, every time Anastasia rose to help her, the dark, locked box in her mind came with her. Lana couldn't have Anastasia's help without all those dark emotions—her fears, her grief, her memories—coming along for the ride.

Lana straightened up and wrapped her hand around the hilt of her sword in the same way she'd seen Alix do so many times before. "You're right."

Alix jerked her head to the side, looking over her shoulder at Lana.

"But I want to be better. Teach me," Lana said.

Alix turned back around and kept walking as she barked out a dry laugh. "Yeah?"

"I'm serious. Please," Lana said.

Alix looked up and pressed her hand into her wound. "All right. Sure. I don't know how I'm supposed to teach you to have a backbone, but perhaps you can learn."

"Thank you," Lana whispered.

"The only advice I'll give you right now is this: trust yourself. A hesitant sword is dead."

How could she trust herself? She wasn't a knight—Anastasia was. Lana frowned and followed silently as they moved through the hallways, staring intently at the back of Alix's head in the dimness, barely lit by moss-torches.

Lana was still staring when they took a flight of stairs up and broke back into the surface of the city. The city air was fresher than the den, but only just barely. Lana turned around in a circle, taking in the view of the desolate city. Meredith limped ahead of them, but her bleeding had completely stopped. Now Alix was the one who needed help. Blood soaked through her makeshift bandages and dripped down her sides. There was no way they would find Remi in time to matter.

Alix hunched by the entryway that they had just exited from. Labored breaths escaped her lips as she pressed her hand to her wound. The bleeding hadn't stopped. Her face was paler than it should be. She stood up, pushing away from the wall with a stagger. "Come on." She took a few steps away from the wall.

"There's got to be something else to do. Some other way. You won't make it through the city without collapsing. I can't carry you. I can't do this. How am I supposed to find him? I don't know what to do." Lana's voice shifted a pitch up.

"We do what we have to do." Alix forced herself to stand taller. The fabric across Alix's wound was falling away again, just enough that Lana could see the top of the wound.

Lana's eyes widened. The wound was closing itself up, slowly. Tiny red vines, like the ones all the Hollows wore, threaded across her flesh at a snail's pace. Impossibly slow, almost imperceptible, but Lana saw it.

Alix trudged along the path, using the nearby buildings for support. Her eyes were on the city, seeking with hawk-like alertness for some sign of her soldiers. She moved with purpose.

Lana's eyes never left those red vines on Alix's flesh. "What happened to you?"

Alix clenched her free hand, but didn't stop moving. "What are you talking about?"

The familiar golden glow of Anastasia bubbled to the surface, and a wave of tears followed. "What happened? You were hunting them and now you wear the vines and nurse their queen to health? Meredith betrayed you. She betrayed both of us and sided with the monsters that killed *my* people!" Pain, like open flames, seared her throat. Lana lost her grip on Liam and he slid to the ground at her feet. She grabbed at her throat, struggling against the burning tightness that flooded her body like a tidal wave of rage.

Alix turned, ready with a scowl, but halted as her eyes landed on Lana, whose eyes were a golden light. Anastasia's eyes. Alix's face dropped, and she turned away again, closing her eyes as she leaned against the stone wall.

Meredith stood off to the side, quiet and watchful.

"You know what she is to me. You remember what it was like when I lost her—when I thought I lost her..." Alix pressed a hand to her eyelids. "I thought she would be better off dead than Hollow—maybe she still would be. Maybe they'd all be better off, but... I can't lose her again."

Lana gasped for air as Anastasia spoke through her again. "She abandoned you. Rejected you. The Hollows are a blight," she spat, clenching her fists. Lana shivered. Anastasia's presence was all-consuming. She pressed up against Lana's mind. The golden glow surged within her, threatening to take complete control.

"Enough," Alix said.

"I will say when enough is enough, General." Anastasia's voice spilled from her throat again and she grabbed Alix's shoulder roughly.

Alix grimaced, turning her head to glare down at Lana, who was held captive by Anastasia's spirit.

"I died to save you and the rest of the Silvids," Anastasia said.

"No. You never died. They wouldn't let you. The Silvids are beyond saving, and you know that. You knew that then."

"What did you expect me to do?!" Anastasia's grip tightened on Alix's shoulder.

Alix's knees buckled, and she sank down onto her knees to escape the ache of Anastasia's grip. "Stay and fight like we always did." Alix's eyes were fierce.

"It was hopeless. There was no way to defeat them. That was the best we could hope for, to trap them on the island."

"It was never hopeless. When the prince disappeared, you just gave up." Alix spat the words with an accusing glare. "You were the hope of Haven. You were practically suicidal, so Haven gave up. I have every intention of finishing this fight, but now that I have Meredith back, I'm not letting her go."

Alix lowered her voice and grabbed Anastasia's hand. "You understand that, right? I can't live without her."

Anastasia's eyes softened. She understood. Anastasia didn't want to lose anyone else ever again either.

"Are you going to stand by my side again in our war?" Alix asked.

Anastasia dropped her eyes. Whatever her mother had done had broken her in some way she couldn't fathom. It felt like a piece of her was missing, a shard of her existence separate from herself. "I can't. My soul is shattered and lost. I can't control my magic. I can't be of use," Anastasia said, suppressing a sob at the admission.

"What do you think you're doing now? Reminiscing?" Alix laughed coldly.

Anastasia looked down at her hand, that was still clamped on Alix's shoulder. Her hand was glowing bright gold. She yanked it away from Alix and choked as she saw the burned flesh underneath.

"I'm sorry."

"No. Don't apologize. Do something. Stop playing and do something. Face this."

"I don't know what to do. I'm not myself. Something's not right." The golden glow dimmed in Anastasia's eyes.

Anastasia blinked, a wave of dizziness washing over her as she faded, feeling Lana's return to consciousness. Her vision darkened at the edges, and heat rose in her body until the world went dark and disappeared. *Alone.* In a vast abyss of nothing, Lana stood and Anastasia stared back.

CHAPTER 22

Lana

In the darkness, they stared at each other. Amber eyes met chocolate brown. So much alike. All their memories rushed together as they gazed into each other's eyes. Anastasia's childhood in Haven, fighting with the Hollows, her friends, her family, meeting Vas and then losing him. Where Anastasia's memories left off, Lana's picked up. Her entire life flashed before her eyes—her childhood with Liam, her father's death, their families, her coworkers at Mina's, her mother's disappearance, the nightmares, losing Marty to his fears, losing Liam. Every moment since then.

They had been happy, grieving, scared, confused. All the emotions rolled through her at once, and Lana sobbed, finally letting tears drip down her cheeks as the ache squeezed her heart. Anastasia grabbed Lana's hand until her sobs slowed, and once again they stood in silence in the darkness together.

"Where are we?" Lana wiped her face against the sleeve of her shirt.

"An in-between place of our souls, somewhere inside our minds, most likely."

Anastasia smiled, and it felt familiar to Lana. The edges of her own lips curved upward, turning her countenance into a mirror of Anastasia's.

"None of this has made sense from the moment I woke up here," Lana said.

Anastasia nodded. "I think our mother has the answers."

"Me too, but I don't know how to find her."

Anastasia shrugged. "Me neither, but we've got to work together to find her and to find the answers. I can't exist without you."

"But," Lana said, letting words rush from her lips, "you come to the surface, and it's fine. You took control. You can do that. I'm nothing. I'm useless. I can't help them. They need you. I don't have any magic. This is your body."

Anastasia shook her head and squeezed Lana's hand. "Magic may live in the body, but it comes from the soul. I need you to help me. They need us. I'm not whole. I can't keep coming to the surface like that without burning, and when I've tried to work with you...your locked box of emotions..."

"Yeah," Lana said. "I know."

"You can't keep locking them in there. Let's help each other."

Lana shook her head again and tried to pull away from Anastasia, but her grip remained firm, comforting, challenging her to be more than she was.

"I don't know if I can do this."

"You can." Anastasia smiled. "And you won't be alone. We can do this together. We can rescue Vas and find Mom and help the Silvids. Face the parts of life you want to ignore."

Lana squeezed her eyes shut, her heart pounding. She was afraid, just like she always was. She was afraid to take a step, but there was too much on the line for her to just run away again. Lana had to do something. This wasn't about her. She had to do something for everyone else. She had to be brave for them.

Lana opened her eyes and nodded once. "All right. Together."

Anastasia smiled at her. They stood there, holding hands as the darkness faded around them. They were together again when the world came back into view. Though Lana couldn't see Anastasia anymore, she could still feel her presence.

Though all the emotions she'd been running from were at the surface now, it was different than it had been before. Anastasia helped carry that weight, and Lana was lighter. There was comfort in knowing she wasn't alone anymore. She didn't have to be alone anymore.

Anastasia's magic zipped across Lana's skin and she jerked, startled at the sudden energy that buzzed in her veins. She stretched her fingers, laughing as sparks danced across her fingertips.

Finally noticing her surroundings, Lana realized she wasn't alone.

Lana sat on the ground a little way off from the Hollows' den. Liam curled on the ground beside her, and Alix lay nearby on a hastily prepared mat of clothes and a bedroll. Remi kneeled beside her, working on the wound. He wielded magic. The other two knights, whose name Lana had never been told, stood off to the side, watching Remi work.

Silvid magic, Anastasia said in that shared space they now had in their mind.

With each movement of Remi's hand, Alix's wound became less and less, until her skin was smooth and unbroken, though a scar formed.

"What about Meredith?" Lana said.

Remi jolted from surprise, whipping his head around toward Lana. "What?"

"She led us out of the den."

Remi's brows jumped up. "Oh?" He looked back down at Alix, who was barely rousing.

"What happened? How did you find us?" Lana asked.

"I saw the light and knew it could only be you, so I came, hoping to find my general. We weren't far off."

"The light?" Lana furrowed her brow. She didn't remember anything after Anastasia surfaced, and certainly there had been no light.

Remi kept his gaze on Alix as she spoke. "I don't know what happened. When I arrived, you were kneeling in the dirt. Light radiated around you. You were a tiny sun, like a beacon in this endless night. My general collapsed at your feet. Perhaps you can tell me what happened." Remi pushed a strand of hair off Alix's shoulder.

"Anastasia returned." Alix's voice was hoarse, as if she'd been screaming. "I imagine that is what you saw." She pushed herself slowly into a sitting position. "I'm sorry, Remi, that you had to resort to magic."

Remi averted his gaze from Alix. His brows furrowed in confusion, but he didn't question her. He simply nodded in response to Alix.

Alix pierced Lana with her gaze. Her brows jumped up, and she leaned closer. "Your eyes..."

"What?" Lana brushed her fingers against her own eyelids. "Am I bleeding?" Her fingers came away dry.

"Your eyes have gone strange — blended somehow."

Lana's shoulders tightened, and she felt around her eyes again. "What do you mean?"

"Your dark brown is mixed with Anastasia's gold. Your eyes are hazel, now, I guess. Strange."

Lana laughed, dropping her hands from her face. She truly wasn't alone. They were doing this together. From within, Anastasia was at her side, always.

Alix regarded Lana with amusement. "Are you ready to do what needs to be done, then?"

Lana nodded. "We're ready." Anastasia's eagerness flooded her mind, bringing an odd smile to Lana's face — a lopsided, nervous smile.

"Then here's my plan." Alix pushed up to her feet, stretching out her muscles. She moved slowly, but otherwise seemed as if she'd never been injured. "Athan has his own fort on the outskirts of Haven, deep in the side caverns. We'll need more than just us, but the unconscious boy is a burden. So Remi and the knights will take the boy to Elaine's house. I'll find Meredith—she must have found somewhere safe before you exploded into light," she said with narrowed eyes at Lana. "You should find Shiloh. He said he'd look for enchanted tools from Elaine, right? He might have found something we can use—at the very least, he's a mage, which will come in handy. We'll rendezvous here in two hours, regardless of whether we've found them."

Lana's heart raced. "You mean for me to go alone?"

"It's not far." Alix scanned across the city. "And Anastasia is with you now, right? She can handle the city."

Lana shifted uneasily.

Alix laughed. "It won't be long."

"Then why don't I just go with you?"

"We don't have enough time. The longer we wait, the higher the chance Athan will devise some escape. Not to mention your prince is still with him."

Her heart twisted at the reminder. Vas — her new friend, her sister's love, and the other half of Liam's soul — was trapped with Athan. She would do what she must. Lana nodded. "All right."

Then, without another word, they dispersed, leaving Lana alone in the plaza. She turned toward the city, looking out into the empty stretch that glowed faintly with bioluminescent blue, a foreign skyline of shadows, where the Hollows lurked, waiting for her. With a deep breath, she stepped onto the path, alone for the first time since leaving her human home so many nights ago.

CHAPTER 23

Luze

Sprawled in the comfort of a familiar bed, Luze opened his eyes, blinking away the remnants of one of Athan's sleep spells. He rubbed at his cheeks and mentally checked his body for injuries. Nothing. His mind subconsciously wrapped around the golden thread of his mate bond—thin, but unbroken. He felt nothing through the bond, which was normal, considering the bond hadn't quite snapped into place. His mate didn't know, and he intended to keep it that way, at least for a little while longer. *As long as he didn't know, he couldn't reject him.*

He sighed, clutching at his shirt above his heart. At least it wasn't broken. He sat up and took stock of his surroundings. A fire crackled in a fireplace at the far end of the one-room cottage. He knew exactly where he was—the mushroom garden west of Haven. He and Athan spent a summer here when they first escaped Brynia, before they began working in the Silvid Court.

Everything looked the same as it had. A small table sat in front of the fire, which had a bubbling cauldron hanging over it. The earthy smell of mushroom soup filled the small room as it warmed over the fire. A brown, patchwork rug covered the wooden floor near the bed, which was the only furniture in the room besides the table, dish cabinet, and wardrobe.

On the rug, the prince curled in on himself in silence, looking much more like the child Luze remembered from so long ago—sorrowful and alone. Luze frowned. *What had happened? Was he okay?* Luze slid from the bed to the floor, quietly making his way to Vas's side.

Vas's chest rose and fell with breath. He was merely sleeping, but worry gnawed at Luze's mind. Athan surely wouldn't hurt the prince. Back at the palace, he had cared so much for the little prince—just like Athan had cared for Luze when they were children. The sound of snapping leather still made Athan flinch after all the beatings he'd taken in Luze's stead.

But Athan had changed in these twenty years.

Luze hated using the sense magic spell—it was disorienting and uncomfortable, but he needed to make sure there wasn't some malicious spell keeping him in slumber.

Luze closed his eyes and focused on the pulse of magic around him. The fire at the far end of the room roared with energy, potent and flickering. He lifted his hand and called that energy to him; it filled him, pulsing and pounding. Luze gasped for breath. He'd never been talented with magic, but nevertheless, he forced himself to continue.

The magical energy vibrated with raw heat beneath his skin. He took hold of it and channeled it through his words—"*beseo ielfsiden,*" Luze said. In a rush, the magic hummed and circled his eyes. The sensation was awful. How his brother kept this spell going at all times, he never understood.

When he opened his eyes, magic, like transparent multicolored smoke, swirled around the room and pulsed in everything around him. In some places it was dim, nearly nonexistent—like the old, dead wood of the floors or the fibers of the rug—but in others it was nearly blinding. The prince was one of those blinding spots.

Luze narrowed his eyes as he looked down at Vas. He'd always been a soul brimming with magic, but this was significantly more energy than Luze remembered from the one time Athan had insisted he look at the prince with the spell active. *What happened? Was this the wellspring?* Raw magic thrummed through Vas, swirling and pulsating, pushing at his skin. Luze took a shuddering breath and refocused on his task—checking for any magic not belonging to Vas—but there was nothing. *Was he in pain?*

Luze couldn't bear the buzzing in his eyes. No magic influenced the prince, so Luze quickly dissolved the spell with a muttered word—"*Tofaran.*"

"Vas?" Luze asked, daring a hand on the prince's shoulder. Vas opened his eyes, which were rimmed with red, making the green seem even brighter than it normally was. "What's wrong?"

After a long moment of silence, with the prince staring up at Luze with sorrow plain on his face, Vas sat up and told Luze what happened and about the changeling who had lived in the mundane world with Lana.

Luze listened quietly to Vas's tale. He looked so much like his father, the king, that Luze couldn't help but pat the prince's hand to comfort him—the boy who had lost so much.

"Athan wants to get rid of Lana and my changeling. He's trapped us here. I can't do anything," Vas said. "I've already tried to leave, but there's a barrier around the cottage."

Luze tapped a finger on his lips. With Vas's magical power, no barrier could hold him back. "What have you tried?"

Vas bit at his lip. "Well, I never learned much magic beyond some illusions." He dropped his gaze to the floor and wrapped his arms around his knees. "I've tried forcing my way through it, clawing through it, but I don't know what else." He huffed out a frustrated breath and whispered, "I was such an idiot back then, so focused on trying to conceal my horns that I didn't care to learn anything else."

"An easy enough fix," Luze laughed. Oh, he would enjoy seeing Athan's face when he realized he had underestimated them. With Luze's knowledge and Vas's strength, they would get out of this place with ease.

Just outside the window, a golden light lit the cavern. Vas and Luze's attention snapped to Haven, where a beam of sunshine erupted from the city center. Vas rushed to the window, clinging to the frame as he watched the beacon as it slowly fizzled out.

"Lana." Vas gasped and dropped to his knees by the window, clutching his chest.

Luze kneeled beside him, watching with wide-eyed panic. *What was he supposed to do? What happened?*

After a tense moment, Vas exhaled. His body visibly relaxed. "We have to get out of here. I need to get to her."

"And you will." Luze offered his hand to help the prince to his feet. "I'll teach you how to break spells."

Luze and Vas made their way to the cottage door, determined to escape Athan's trap.

CHAPTER 24

Lana

Following the road to her father's abandoned house, Lana felt eyes on her from the rooftops and the shadowy windows. The weight of their gaze fell on her, but she didn't understand why the creatures hadn't slunk from their hiding spots to tear her apart. *Did Athan have that much power over them? Had he ordered them not to harm her? Or were they afraid of her?*

She hoped they were afraid. Anastasia's light must have been incredible. Without trying, the magic rose to the surface, and flames ran down her arms before forming small spheres of golden fire in her hand. The flames danced there for a moment, and Lana laughed at the ease she called them up now, but even now, she could feel the drain inside her as the magic pulled from Anastasia's shattered soul.

She manipulated the flame, watching it writhe and dance in her hand before extinguishing it. She would need to be careful not to use the magic too much, but she wasn't helpless anymore.

Confidence made her unguarded. Shiloh took her by surprise as he lurched into view. He looked hellish, with tattered clothes covered in blood and soot. Before she could react, his hands dug into her arms, his eyes wide with panic.

Fear swelled in her chest and she scrambled, trying to push him away, to wriggle free, but Shiloh held on as he babbled with a trembling voice.

"I can't find him. Athan has taken him somewhere. He's gone and the amulet—the amulet!" He jerked away and cradled something to his chest. "It's broken! Hopeless. It's hopeless. I found it. I found a tracker, but none of it works."

"Shi. What's wrong?"

"Ana," he sobbed. "I'm so sorry. I've ruined everything."

"Just take a moment. What's going on?"

"Luze is gone," he said.

"Gone?"

"After you left with Bludeg, I went to Elaine's library in Creon's house and I found the amulet. I found so much—a treasure trove of magical items, like this tracker and the amulet, but then..." His eyes flashed with anger, face twisting with barely restrained rage. "Athan destroyed everything. Luze is gone, and the amulet shattered. If we can't find Elaine, if she's dead, if she can't undo what's been done, you'll only ever be half a soul—a broken piece of what you once were."

Shiloh fisted his hands around the objects. "I can't even get the tracker to work to find Luze. He's gone." He shoved the compass-like object in her direction, pointing at the needle that swung back and forth between two points.

The two points weren't in opposite directions. One pointed just south, toward the mushroom forest outside of Haven, and the other pointed in the direction she came from—back to the plaza, where she would meet back with Alix. "Let's just follow this one." She indicated the one that pointed back to city hall. In his current state, she didn't want to mention yet that she needed his help. Hopefully, Alix could handle that part.

Shiloh nodded, clutching at the compass. He started down the road, not waiting for her to follow. It wasn't long before they stood in the plaza again.

She expected to see Alix, or even Remi and the soldiers, but instead, Luze stood before her with a Cheshire grin.

"Oh, hey." Lana smiled back at Luze, even though something about his grin made her uneasy.

Relief had Shiloh sagging and rushing forward, but he halted, looking down at the compass and back up to Luze with a furrowed brow. His eyes caught on Luze's face, lingering on the sharpness of his grin.

"Something's not right." Shiloh tried to pull Lana away.

Lana jerked from his grasp. "What are you talking about? We found Luze. Have you completely lost it?"

Luze clasped his hands together in front of him and nodded. "Wonderful. What perfect timing. I was just looking for you."

"So was Shiloh, but his compass is acting weird. Alix and the others should be here soon. I need your help to rescue Vas. I need help from both of you," Lana said, ignoring Shiloh's pleading at her side.

Luze's eyebrows raised as his eyes widened slightly. "Alix and her soldiers?" He paused for a moment, and his face slid back into its usual careful expression. "Athan's fort is deep in the outer caves and guarded on all sides. An entire party of armed soldiers, loud and aggressive, is not the way to go. You need stealth to take your prince back."

Lana twisted her lips to either side as she thought. He had a point, but there was no way she could go alone. She wouldn't survive. Even with Anastasia's strength and magic at her command, she couldn't save him alone.

"I could go with you." Luze's voice was barely above a whisper. "Between the two of us, we could certainly slip in and slip out, with no one the wiser."

Lana tilted her head to the side in thought, regarding him carefully. The gentle breeze of the cavern brushed across Lana's face, bringing with it the lingering stench of the Hollows.

"Lana, please," Shiloh muttered. "Don't listen to him. I can't fight him again." He pulled at her sleeve, tugging with the insistence of insanity.

She wondered what scheme Shiloh was trying this time. She didn't trust him anymore, shouldn't have trusted him in the first place.

"And I certainly know the caves better than the soldiers would. I've lived here with Shiloh for quite a long time," Luze said.

His offer was enticing. She didn't want to burden Alix anymore, either. She'd already done so much. Lana opened her mouth to agree, but shook her head. "Alix will come in after us."

"Oh, that won't be a problem," Luze replied. "At best, they'll be a distraction so we can slip inside. At worst, they'll get lost and never find the fort."

Lana shook her head again. "No. I'll wait and at least talk to them first. I'm sure Alix will agree after I've explained it to her."

Luze pursed his lips. "Is she really so reasonable? She will let you wander into the dark with only me as your guide? You know she likes to control things far too much. Just come on."

"Lana," Shiloh whispered, his gaze moving quickly between the compass in his hand and the man standing before him.

Luze reached out toward her, but Lana stepped back away from him, pulling her arm from his reach.

"No. I think she'll know it's a better plan. We'll talk it out and figure out the best course of action. I want to talk to Alix first." Lana felt relieved as she saw the familiar silhouettes of Alix and Meredith on the top of the hill. They would be here in minutes. Luze was acting strangely. He'd never been warm or friendly, but something about him today put her on edge. Or perhaps it was just Shiloh's muttering and panic getting to her.

Luze spotted Alix in the distance and cursed. "I really had hoped to be a bit nicer with this, or perhaps a bit crueler, to have some fun. Ah well." He sighed and stepped toward her. "It can't be helped."

She watched in horror as Luze's figure swirled in smoke and purple flashes. His face melted away in a fog, revealing a new grin. Anastasia's shaking voice dominated Lana's thoughts. *Athan shouldn't be able to do that. Shifting like that is just a myth.*

Athan laughed. "Did you think illusions couldn't be this good?" He tossed a wide grin toward Shiloh, who stood at Lana's side. "After all, I'm just an unpredictable shapeshifter, right, Shi?" He cackled again as wings formed on his back, ready to lift him into the air.

Shiloh trembled and held out his hands. Flames shot in a circle around them, straight up to the cavernous ceiling. "Tell me what you have done with Luze. I won't let you get away this time!" Shiloh screamed, smoke streaming from his lips with each word, covering his face with the ashes.

If he kept pushing himself like this, especially after whatever happened before, he would die. "Shiloh. You're going to burn!" Lana shouted, but Shiloh shook his head.

"Either way, we're probably both dead." He stared intently at the monster that was Athan.

He could make his own choices, so instead of begging Shiloh to release the magic burning through his soul, she turned her anger on Athan. As she pulled the sword from her sheath, fire ran along the blade, coaxed into existence by Anastasia's magic.

"You're not going anywhere!" Letting her rage fuel her, Lana ran and leaped into the air, plunging her sword into Athan's side. They collided and fell to the ground.

Lana shuddered as she felt his vines wrapping up her leg and spread across her chest, but this time Athan had no help from the Hollows and Lana wasn't alone. The Keeper's flame burned across her skin, scorching the vines where they touched.

Athan screamed and jerked away, rolling along the ground to put out the flames. When he stood, she was ready for him. Fire met shadow. He grit his teeth, wild red eyes staring down at her. He lunged. Lana dodged away, out of reach of his grasp, but his magic was already coming. Red vines rolled in waves along the ground, questing and seeking for her flesh.

Meredith and Alix, along with the three other soldiers, broke through Shiloh's ring of fire. Athan glared at the newcomers, letting his vines spread toward them.

Meredith straightened and stretched her hands out in front of her. Her fingers elongated into gruesome claws, wriggling with red vines. She rolled her shoulders, and they buckled, making a sickening pop as her body disfigured itself, growing and moving into a new shape.

Athan cackled. "It really is a shame how difficult it is for you to do what comes so easy for a Brynian. No amount of magic siphoned from the source can replace what is born in my blood."

With his words, Athan shifted. It had taken Meredith nearly a minute to shift only part of herself into a gruesome creature of fang, tooth, and bone, wrapped in vines and magic. It took seconds for Athan to shift in a whirl of fog. He stepped toward Meredith on strong paws, wrapped in red vines.

Once again, he was a panther, pure predator and instinct.

Athan and Meredith fell upon each other. They grappled, rolling to the ground in a flurry of teeth and claw. Even with Shiloh's magic, Lana, Alix, and her soldiers to distract him, Meredith was barely holding her own against Athan. Over and over again, their bodies slammed against each other, claws raking into flesh. Though Athan fought Meredith, his magic still tormented the rest—stones flying through the air, water and wind pulling at them.

He was too powerful. Lana moved carefully around the edge of the battle, watching for her opening. Athan sank his fangs into Meredith's shoulder and shook, throwing her aside. She crumpled against the ground and didn't move. Alix rushed to her side.

Athan shifted. As a man once again, he grinned, laughing at his supposed triumph.

This was it. This was her opening.

Lana rushed in and sank her sword into his back. His flesh squelched, and Athan gasped. He turned toward her as he pulled the blade from his flesh. The Hollow vines were already mending his wound. Before Lana realized what was happening, Athan's body was against her. Pain ripped through her chest. He had buried her own sword in her chest with one hand, and held her close to him with the other.

"How?" Lana could barely speak past the pain.

He twisted the blade, rocking it side to side, causing new blooms of pain. She was having trouble breathing. Athan yanked the sword from her chest and pushed her down toward the ground.

A shout pierced the air as Shiloh ran toward Lana's falling figure. She hit the ground hard, gasping and choking on her own blood. Their blood. Anastasia's blood. The world grew dark, the fighting muffled.

Remi's face came into view, and his hands moved quickly over her body. She had given up once before. She wouldn't accept defeat. Remi's magic mixed with her own golden flames, heating and moving, sewing the rips in her flesh. In the haze of pain and blood loss, she watched the battle continue without her.

Athan was on the ground, dark blood dripping from his torn wings, throwing magic in all directions. Alix and her soldiers surrounded him on all sides, keeping pressure as they dodged his shadowy vines. At the edge of the fray, Shiloh stood with flames pouring from his hands and mouth, black ash smeared across his face. Golden light rained down on Athan and singed his flesh.

They still had a chance. They could defeat him. A victorious glee rushed through Lana, but it was premature.

Athan roared and threw his hands in the air as stone pillars shot from the ground, tossing the soldiers to the side. Athan hissed, now wielding water and stone against the flame and swords.

"Hello, brother."

Lana's head swam as she looked toward the voice that had stepped into the edge of the battle — Luze and Vas.

"No!" Athan shouted, lunging toward Luze.

But Shiloh threw up a wall of molten gold that burned Athan wherever it landed. Athan muttered, casting a barrier that encircled him, protecting him from Shiloh's fiery magic, which wavered as Shiloh swayed like a branch in a rough wind.

Athan grinned as he stepped forward with his magical barrier.

Vas stood beside Luze, his own ghostly purple magic swirling at his feet. Vas spoke—*"Tofaran"*—and, in a sudden pop of purple light, Athan's barrier dissolved.

"What?" Athan blinked in surprise. The last of Shiloh's flickering flames burned across Athan's skin, and he jerked away as the flames sputtered out and Shiloh fell to his knees. A spear zinged through the air, thrown by one of Alix's soldiers, but before Athan could put up his shield again, Vas was already ready to break it. The spear tip slashed against Athan's side, cutting deep.

Athan scanned the battlefield. Blood dripped from his wounds and his body slumped with exhaustion, though his eyes softened, a pleased smile on his lips, as he turned to Vas.

"Vasileios, you've done well," he said. "But I need you to know that nothing that I've told you has been a lie, though they may try to convince you otherwise." The warriors circled him, stalking closer with each word he spoke. "I kept you safe. I want to return you to yourself — whole, unbroken without the obstacle of your changeling. I want to help you, to help you rule Silvis and make it the safest court in all of Kaelum. You understand, don't you?"

Vas lifted his chin, refusing to answer him.

Athan's eyes glistened, catching the mosslight for the briefest moment before a plume of purple smoke exploded and the earth rumbled. Athan disappeared, leaving only the echo of his parting words: "When you're ready to rise to your true potential, I will be waiting."

The battle was over, but the war had barely begun.

CHAPTER 25

Lana

In the bloody aftermath of the battle, Remi and Alix hovered over Meredith. Luze and Shiloh sat on the ground, talking in whispers. Even though Remi had closed the wound, stitching together the place where Athan had punctured her lung, the pain surged through her chest when she tried to move. But somehow, they all made it back to her mother's house. Everyone else soon washed and sought out somewhere to rest. It had been an excruciatingly long day.

Vas lingered in the main room, watching Lana. "Thank you," he said.

Lana raised a brow. "I should be thanking you and Luze."

He tilted his head to the side with a playful grin. "I guess we should call it even then? You came to save me in the Hollow den and I came for you."

"Yes. We're even." Lana matched his grin with a tired one of her own. She didn't know what to think, knowing that Vas and Liam shared the same soul. It felt different being around him now. Each movement he made seemed more familiar. But what did that mean for Liam? Would he never wake? She frowned.

The mood shifted, as if the air between them had suddenly cooled. Vas ruffled his hair and cast his eyes to the floor. A slight frown pulled at his lips. "I'll let you rest. Goodnight."

Lana pursed her lips. Had she said the wrong thing? "Goodnight," she called after him as he wandered down the hall and into a bedroom.

She desperately wanted to sleep too, but her mind kept going back to Liam. Despite her exhaustion, Lana sought him out. Remi had brought Liam to the house after the incident in the Hollow den and put him in one of the downstairs bedrooms. She crept into Liam's room. A mosslight lamp glowed gently on a nearby desk, illuminating the room with the now-familiar blue glow.

He rested peacefully on the bed, tucked in and relaxed. His dark hair haloed his face in a mess of waves. Standing beside him, Lana couldn't help but take his hand. Her fingers intertwined with his, just like they used to when they were kids, hiding under blankets after watching scary movies. His mom always warned us off the movies, but it never stopped them. She squeezed his fingers.

His fingers wrapped around hers tighter, squeezing ever so slightly.

Lana held her breath. "Liam?"

His eyelids fluttered, then opened.

"Liam?"

He blinked slowly. His green stare found hers and he smiled. That bright smile, familiar and comforting warmed her, and Lana collapsed beside his bed, reaching for him. Tears burned in her eyes.

He twisted, pulling her into an embrace. "Lana, what's wrong?"

"I'm so glad you're awake," she said, shuddering.

Luze peeked into the room. "I'm sorry to interrupt, but we have a problem."

Lana tightened her grip on Liam, burying her face in the familiar scent of his embrace. She didn't want to hear whatever awful thing Luze had to say. She just wanted this moment with Liam, but his voice cut through her relief at Liam's awakening.

"Lana's body is missing."

Liam is finally awake, but Vas still hasn't told Lana the truth about his fated mate. What will happen when she finds out that she might just be Vas's mate?

Find Out What Happens Next: Read More https://books2read.com/Mosslight

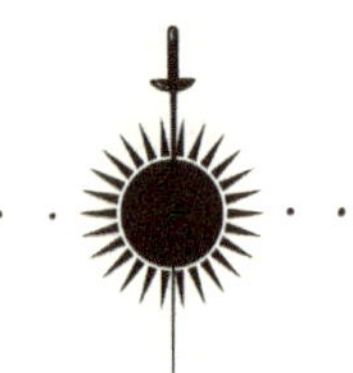

Join the Faerie Friends Newsletter for updates on new releases, sales, and behind-the-scenes fun from A.J. Nora. When you sign up, you get a **BONUS** scene!

Read now for free: https://dashboard.mailerlite.com/forms/1224485/158024175059994284/share

Thank you so much for reading! As an indie author, your support means everything to me. Without you, I wouldn't be able to continue writing the stories I love. If you'd like to help others fall in love with this story too, please consider leaving a review and telling your friends!

Here are some helpful links to show your support:

Review: https://www.goodreads.com/book/show/2424 04563-of-dreams-and-mosslight

Join the Newsletter: https://dashboard.mailerlite.com/fo rms/1224485/158024175059994284/share

Follow me on social media: https://ajnorabooks.com/soc ials

About the Author

A.J. Nora is a queer author from the deep south, who writes epic fantasy with romance. She loves swords and magic, fated mates, and faerie royalty. She became obsessed with faeries after reading the Fae Fever series when she was in high school. Ever since then, she's been writing down her daydreams, hoping to share them with the world.

If you'd like to come along on her indie author journey, follow A.J. on social media:

Join the Newsletter for book updates, sales, and exclusive stories:

https://dashboard.mailerlite.com/forms/1224485/140523304324695307/share

Facebook : https://m.facebook.com/61561948896462/

Instagram: https://www.instagram.com/ajnorabooks/

TikTok: https://www.tiktok.com/@ajnorabooks

Bluesky: https://bsky.app/profile/ajnorabooks.bsky.social

Tumblr: https://www.tumblr.com/ajnorabooks